THE FORGOTTEN

PREVIOUS BOOKS BY ALAN REFKIN

FICTION

Matt Moretti and Han Li Series

The Archivist
The Abductions
The Payback

Mauro Bruno Detective Series

The Patriarch
The Scion
The Artifact

NONFICTION

The Wild Wild East: Lessons for Success in Business in Contemporary Capitalist China
By Alan Refkin and Daniel Borgia, PhD

Doing the China Tango: How to Dance around Common Pitfalls in Chinese Business Relationships
By Alan Refkin and Scott Cray

Conducting Business in the Land of the Dragon: What Every Businessperson Needs To Know About China
By Alan Refkin and Scott Cray

Piercing the Great Wall of Corporate China: How to Perform Forensic Due Diligence on Chinese Companies
By Alan Refkin and David Dodge

THE FORGOTTEN

A MATT MORETTI AND HAN LI THRILLER

ALAN REFKIN

THE FORGOTTEN
A MATT MORETTI AND HAN LI THRILLER

iUniverse books may be ordered through booksellers or by contacting:

iUniverse
1663 Liberty Drive
Bloomington, IN 47403
www.iuniverse.com
844-349-9409

Because of the dynamic nature of the Internet, any web addresses or links contained in this book may have changed since publication and may no longer be valid. The views expressed in this work are solely those of the author and do not necessarily reflect the views of the publisher, and the publisher hereby disclaims any responsibility for them.

Any people depicted in stock imagery provided by Getty Images are models, and such images are being used for illustrative purposes only. Certain stock imagery © Getty Images.

ISBN: 978-1-6632-2096-7 (sc)
ISBN: 978-1-6632-2097-4 (e)

Library of Congress Control Number: 2021907246

Print information available on the last page.

iUniverse rev. date: 04/08/2021

To my wife Kerry, my best friend and compass in our journey through life.

To Wings of Shelter

PROLOGUE

Present Day-Santorini, Greece

Moretti and Han Li raced towards their room at the Mystique Hotel, hurrying down the steep winding steps carved into the side of the caldera. With only a minute or two lead over Tosku's men, they wished they could go to the airport and let security protect them. That meant leaving the flash drive that Moretti caulked to the underside of one of their hotel windows. Failure to retrieve it would affect the lives of thousands. That wasn't an option.

Hanging out a window 1,000 feet above the jagged volcanic rocks piercing the sea below, Moretti ripped the caulk away from the flash drive and stuffed it into his pants pocket. As he was doing this, Han Li grabbed whatever she could and threw it into their carry-on bags. It took fifteen seconds to bolt down the steps and thirty to retrieve the drive. It would take twenty seconds to return to the taxi waiting for them on the street above—one minute and five seconds total for the round trip. However, as they were rushing about, neither bothered to look out the large window that faced the placid turquoise waters of the Aegean Sea. If they had, they would have seen a fifty-foot-long boat named the *Hercules* that was half a mile away. They would also have seen several men removing the large blue tarp that was covering a BGM-71 TOW missile and, moments later, the elongated yellow and red flame that shot from the rear as it streaked towards them.

A TOW missile isn't fast but, when its target was eight-tenths of a mile away, it didn't have to be. Five seconds after it left the launcher, it impacted Moretti and Han Li's room - disintegrating it and three rooms on either side. Tons of debris etched out of the caldera rained down on the volcanic rocks below. Witnesses sitting at the Mystique's outdoor restaurant situated a couple of hundred yards from the site of the impact saw the explosion and ensuing fireball - their proximity so close they became singed by the heat and subject to the rain of debris. Most suffered bumps and bruises as they ran for cover. When questioned by authorities, each reported they hadn't seen anyone on the stairs outside the now nonexistent rooms before the fireball. In the end, two hotel guests were unaccounted for and presumed dead.

CHAPTER 1

Five days earlier-Athens, Greece

ATTHEW MORETTI AND Han Li were the first to disembark the Air China flight from Beijing to Athens, their first-class passage paid for by the Chinese government to recognize their heroic actions in stopping terrorists from detonating nuclear devices in Beijing and Shanghai.

A representative of the Grande Bretagne Hotel met them at the aircraft door. The stately-looking man took their carry-on bags and guided them to a VIP line, through customs, and out of the main terminal where a Mercedes S550 was waiting.

Han Li was five feet, eleven inches tall, with an athletic build, black opal-colored eyes, porcelain-like skin, and long brunette hair. She was in her late 20s and had a resonant voice that made her sound like Angelina Jolie. When she walked through the airport, every man's head turned to admire the beautiful Asian. Although the common assumption was that such a tall and stunning woman must be a model, she was formerly China's premier assassin.

Matt Moretti was six feet, three inches tall, and weighed 230 pounds. An ex-Army Ranger in his mid-thirties, he had a chisel-cut face, a thick-chested and muscular physique, cropped black hair, and hazel eyes. While Moretti was the duo's better marksperson, Han Li was a martial arts expert without a peer. Both were members of a clandestine United States-China off-the-books organization known as Nemesis. Formed by both countries' presidents to circumvent bureaucracy's indecisiveness, this elite force was administratively directed by Lieutenant Colonel Doug Cray and operationally commanded by Moretti. Its mandate was to protect both homelands from harm by any means necessary. As a cover, its members worked for a fictional organization known as the White House Statistical Analysis Division, which was accountable only to the president and headquartered at the Raven Rock Mountain Complex in Maryland, also known as Site R. The inquiring minds of those entrenched in Washington bureaucracy believed they were a group of geeks and bean counters who provided data to POTUS who operated out of surplus government space.

They were in Athens because China's President Liu told Moretti and Han Li that they were being given a vacation, not only to recharge their batteries after almost being incinerated in a mine fire following a nuclear explosion but also as a reward for preventing a nuclear holocaust and saving the lives of millions. However, he had a secondary reason for this vacation. After hearing from Yan He, a PLA lieutenant colonel and member of Nemesis, that Moretti had wanted a closer relationship with Han Li for some time but didn't have the courage to ask her out, much less invite her for an overnight trip, he intervened and gave them a chance to determine if there was more to their relationship than business.

With President Liu giving them the option to go anywhere in the world, Han Li suggested Greece. She'd always wanted to see Athens because of the history associated with the city. Moretti agreed. He would go to Newark, New Jersey, if it meant that he got to spend time with her.

It was a 40-minute ride from the airport to central Athens. When they arrived, the representative escorted them to the registration desk, where they discovered the hotel had received payment for a one-bedroom suite for the length of their stay. The hotel manager, who handled the check-in, gave Han Li a large envelope and two key cards at the end of the process. Opening it, she found a Chinese government credit card in her name, a packet of Euros, and a handwritten note from President Liu saying she and Moretti should have a good time and "not overthink the situation."

A bellman accompanied them to their suite and, once he left, the decision was made to unpack later and have a bite to eat at a local restaurant. After getting a recommendation and directions from the concierge, they walked to the Kolonaki area and found the Relanti, a small and intimate restaurant on a quiet side street. Starting with an appetizer of grilled octopus, followed by fresh fish, they finished with a cup of Greek coffee prepared in a small pot called a briki. Although the strong black coffee, with grounds in the cup's bottom and a unique foam on the top, had the consistency of instant coffee-its taste was a universe removed from that, and they both enjoyed a second cup, after which Han Li paid the bill, and they left.

Wanting to sightsee and try a different route back to their hotel, Moretti put the address into an app on his cell phone and, a few seconds later, a map with a blue line appeared - this one showing a different way to return to their hotel. In no hurry, they talked about their childhoods and those who had the greatest influence on their lives. They were so engrossed in their conversation that neither noticed they were the only two people in the area. Han Li was the first to see they were by themselves and commented to Moretti, who looked around and saw the street was a mix of low-end retail interspersed with residences, all on the lower end of the food chain. On the plus side, streetlamps lit the sidewalk, the street, and the alleys that ran perpendicular to it. Moretti looked at his phone and saw they were a quarter mile from the hotel and that the street they were on would intersect the major thoroughfare that would lead them to the front door of the Grande Bretagne.

As they continued to walk, they saw movement in the alley to their right. Running from the shadows into the light was a young girl, in her early teens and weighing no more than 90 pounds, dressed in a filthy shift that was once white but was now charcoal in color. She wore no shoes, and her dark shoulder-length hair was a mass of tangles. Most would have found her face pretty, although a washcloth would have made her even more so. The reason she was running became apparent when the three men chasing her came into view. All had a stocky build, were less than six feet in height, and had thick black stubble on their faces. None brandished a weapon.

Moretti had a Neanderthal approach to anyone trying to chase, harm, or force themselves on females. Once they hit that hot button, the offender had better be carrying more than bad intentions when he encountered the ex-Ranger if he wanted to remain vertical.

As the girl ran into the street, Han Li grabbed her right arm and pulled her aside. Moretti stepped forward and flattened the first two pursuers while the third raced by him and came at the girl. That person, who figured he could take her from the babe, reached for her. However, all he grabbed was air because Han Li extended her right leg and, in the blink of the eye, exercised what in Taekwondo was known as a sewo changi-meaning a vertical kick. His lights were out, and his jaw broken before he hit the ground.

The girl relaxed when she saw her pursuers sprawled on the ground. With Han Li still holding her hand, and without saying a word, they left the unconscious men where they'd fallen and took the girl to their hotel.

"I don't know what that was about," Moretti said once they'd entered the room. "But until we find out, why don't I call room service and get her something to eat while you get her cleaned up. After that, I'll buy her some clothes from whatever shops in the area are open."

"What about calling the authorities?" Han Li asked in a low voice.

"She's dressed like a homeless person and had three men chasing her. I want to find out what this is about before we hand her over to the authorities."

Han Li agreed and, as Moretti was ordering the food, led the girl towards the bathroom.

Thirty minutes later, Moretti returned to find the girl eating steamed sea bass with artichokes, grilled vegetables, and a small Greek salad with feta cheese.

"It looks like you found her some clothes," Han Li said, looking at the two plastic bags in Moretti's hands.

"Don't get too excited; you haven't seen what I bought," he said as he handed the bags to her.

Han Li dumped the contents on the bed, revealing a sweatshirt, pants, three pairs of Crocs, a jacket, and personal items. All except for the shoes had images of the Acropolis imprinted on them. Since Moretti couldn't guess the size of the girl's feet, he'd purchased several pairs of Crocs, hoping one pair would fit.

"I know," he said, seeing the expression on Han Li's face. "This isn't designer-friendly wear. The only stores open are tourist shops. Once she finishes eating, she can change clothes, and we can ask what happened. Maybe there's something we can do to help before we turn her over to the police."

"Don't call the police," the girl said in a voice laced with fear. The response surprised both Moretti and Han Li, not only because they now knew she understood and spoke English, even though her accent carried heavy Slavic undertones, but because she didn't want the police involved.

"Let's start from the beginning," Han Li said in a gentle voice. "My name is Han Li, and this is Matt Moretti. I promise we're going to help you in any way we can and not let anyone harm you. Can you tell us your name?"

"Jehona Dibra."

"How old are you?"

"Fourteen."

"And where are you from, Jehona?" Han Li asked

"Tirana. That's in Albania," she said in a low voice that reflected a bit of shyness.

"Your parents must be worried sick about you."

"They died when I was five. I live in an orphanage. No one will miss me."

The two operatives were at a momentary loss for words until Han Li broke that silence.

"You live in an orphanage?"

"Someone stole me while returning there from school," she answered without emotion.

"Do you know who kidnapped you?" Moretti asked the empathy he felt for the frail teenager apparent in his voice.

She shook her head, indicating that she didn't.

"What happened after they stole you?" Han Li asked, using Jehona's term for kidnapped.

"They forced me to drink some water and threw me into a van, which had sleeping girls inside. When we awoke, we were on a small boat. I was so scared." Jehona said that when the boat docked, they drove her and the other girls to a large house where they slept on cots in a room with other children.

"How long were you in this house?" Han Li asked.

Jehona said she'd lost track of time but that it may have been two to three days.

"That house wasn't in Athens?" Han Li asked.

She said it wasn't.

"Then how did you get here?"

"They put me and some others on another boat."

"And you escaped from there?" Moretti asked.

"I escaped from the building that they took me and the others to."

"Did anyone escape with you?"

Jehona answered she was alone.

"I'm curious," Moretti said. "How were you able to get away?"

"In the evening, we're handcuffed to our cots, after which the guards leave us for the night. I have tiny wrists and slipped out of the cuffs. I found the front door and started running. As soon as I did, three men chased after me. That's when I ran into you."

"You haven't told us why we shouldn't call the police."

"Because I saw men with badges come into the room where we all slept and point to some of the girls. After that, they left with them."

"I understand," Han Li said. "You'll sleep with me tonight. Tomorrow Mr. Moretti and I will see if we can find the building that you mentioned. If we can, we'll tell the police where it is. Most police officers are excellent and will want to help you. I promise until we make sure that you'll be safe, we won't tell anyone about you."

The girl relaxed and went back to eating her food.

"The couch is yours," Han Li said.

"I'm ex-army. This couch is a bed at the Ritz compared to places where I've slept," Moretti replied with a smile. "Tomorrow, I'm going to leave you both for a while."

"And do what?"

"Find the building that Jehona mentioned and interrogate the subhuman assholes who were holding her hostage to see how many other Jehona's there are."

"And after that?"

"I'm going to kill every one of those perverts."

"Do you believe I'm going to let you have all the fun?" Han Li asked.

CHAPTER 2

BEHAR TOSKU WAS handsome. The 41-year-old was six feet, one inch tall, the average height for an Albanian man, and had piercing green eyes. He kept his brown hair short and was an enthusiast of both the sun and a tanning bed, maintaining a medium tan year-round. Clean-shaven and square-jawed, he had a crooked nose after having it broken in several fights and had a steely voice. He was also a psychopath, smuggler, and human trafficker.

He was trying to come to terms with the damage done by the three incompetents standing before him. They'd cost him 100,000 euros by letting the 14-year-old girl escape so that he couldn't deliver her to the buyer who was to arrive later today. He'd decided to get as much mileage out of the situation as possible and reinforce to his men that he would not tolerate failure. With a prearranged signal, he nodded to Bardyhl Gashi - his enforcer who also handled employment issues. The 380 pounds, six feet, seven inches tall bull-necked block of granite pulled a silenced handgun from under his jacket and shot all three men in the back of the head. He then went into the adjoining room, grabbed three black tarps, a couple of duct tape rolls, and began wrapping the bodies for disposal in the furnace that Tosku had in his compound.

"See if any of the hotels in the area have a tall Asian woman staying with a large Caucasian man. If they were walking at night, they're staying in the area. Once you find them, report back to me, and I'll decide how to handle it."

Gashi acknowledged his instructions.

Tosku's enforcer found who he was looking for in the first hotel he tried because the Grande Bretagne was the best place to stay in Athens and a favorite among tourists. Thanks to a bellman who saw the couple and remembered the drop-dead gorgeous Asian, and the well-built Caucasian man with her, Gashi confirmed that the two tourists stayed there and had a girl with them. Since Tosku never used an electronic device for fear that someone in the local or national government would eavesdrop on one of his conversations or hack his computer, he returned to the compound to tell his boss what he'd discovered.

"Put Zika and Vallas on this. Tell them to bring the tourists and the girl here, after which you'll interrogate the tourists to find out what they know and if they've told anyone about the girl. In the meantime, I'll deliver her to the buyer."

Gashi said that he understood and, taking a burner phone from his pocket, called Zika - a number he'd long ago memorized.

Detective Stefan Zika of the Athens General Police Department copied down the information given to him. After telling his partner Dimitri Vallas what Gashi said, they got into their police vehicle and drove to the Grande Bretagne Hotel. Neither had the name of the beautiful Asian woman and the well-built Caucasian man, but they didn't need it, given that the police had the power to access guest records and question the staff at will.

THE FORGOTTEN

The Grande Bretagne was a throwback to the ornateness of luxury accommodations in the mid-nineteenth century. A mansion for a wealthy Greek businessperson, it became a hotel in 1874. In the century and a half that followed, it kept its charm and emphasis on sophisticated elegance. The interior had floors of polished black-and-white marble overlaid at intervals with thick black and gold rugs. White Doric columns were in many interior areas and extended to the high coffered ceilings, outlined by wide white crown molding. The furnishings throughout were late-nineteenth-century antiques that made one feel they stepped back in time.

The two detectives entered the lobby and went to the reception desk. Presenting their credentials, they asked to speak with the manager and, when he arrived, requested the names and room number of the attractive Asian woman who was staying with a Caucasian man. Since the manager had checked Moretti and Han Li into their suite, he gave the detectives what they'd requested and adhered to their warning not to call the room and warn the guests. The two detectives then took the elevator to the seventh floor of the eight-story building.

Moretti answered the knock on the door and saw two medium height and weight men, both with short black hair. Zika, in his late 40s, was the older of the two by five years. He had slate-gray eyes, a large and bulbous nose, and a pockmarked face. His partner had cornflower blue eyes, bushy eyebrows, and a nose inflamed from drinking too much Ouzo in the evening. The team's senior member wore a black suit, a black tie, and a white shirt, while Vallas was more casual and had on a brown tweed jacket and an open-collared

11

dark brown shirt. Both presented their creds and introduced themselves in passable English.

"What can I do for you?" Moretti asked, blocking the doorway and looking Zika in the eye.

"You can turn over the girl you took off the street and come with us to the station to fill out a report."

"Does she have a name?" Moretti asked.

"They didn't give that to us. We were only told that the girl could be a child trafficking victim and to bring her and the two of you to the station. While you complete the necessary paperwork, we'll speak with the girl and start finding her parents. Can we come in?"

Moretti stood aside and let them pass. Once they did, they saw her sitting with Han Li on the couch.

"We know you didn't kidnap her," Vallas said after Moretti let the door close behind them. "A witness said you fought off three men and saved her. They gave us your description, along with that of this attractive lady," Vallas continued, pointing to Han Li. "With that, we could find which hotel you were staying at."

Moretti looked skeptical.

"We didn't see anyone around us, although it's possible someone could have been watching. How do you know she was kidnapped and is a child trafficking victim?" Han Li asked, holding Jehona's hand as she spoke.

"I'm repeating what they told us. Is she family?" Vallas asked.

"No," Han Li replied.

"Then you have no right to keep her here," he said, making a move towards Jehona before Han Li stood and gave him a look that showed she was anything but a helpless female.

"Let's slow down," Moretti said, stepping between them. "What do you plan to do with the girl?"

"We'll take her to the station and begin the process of finding her parents by sending her photo to police departments in neighboring countries to see if someone reported her missing," Zika said.

"Interestingly, you don't believe she's Greek," Han Li said, "as she hasn't spoken a word since you arrived."

"She doesn't look Greek. Is she?" Vallas asked.

Han Li didn't answer. With a statement that surprised everyone, she said: "I believe you're right, detectives. Let's go to the station and get this process started."

Moretti and Han Li sat in the back of the unmarked police car with Jehona. A strong black steel mesh screen separated them from the detectives seated in the front. Moretti tried to open his door but couldn't. Han Li got the same result. Neither was concerned because they were in the back of a police vehicle.

Zika was the driver as the police cruiser left the Grande Bretagne. Weaving through traffic, he entered Highway 64. Twenty minutes later, he transitioned onto Highway 54, passing a sign indicating the vehicle was going towards Rafina. Neither Moretti nor Han Li was familiar with the highways in and around Athens, nor did they know how far the detective's station was from the hotel. Short on patience, Moretti decided they'd been kept in the dark long enough.

"Where are we going, detectives?" Moretti asked in an authoritative voice, starling both Zika and Vallas.

"To our office," Zika replied.

"And where is that?"

"It's not much further. Be patient."

"Why are you investigating an incident in Athens when you're not stationed there?" Moretti asked as he looked out the side window at the coastal road they were on. Neither of the detectives replied, and Zika gave him the finger in response.

Moretti was through talking and, after taking a pen and the receipt for Jehona's clothes from his pocket wrote something on the back and passed it to Han Li. She read it and nodded. What happened next was a blur. Moretti, who sat on the right side of the vehicle, pulled Jehona close to him. As this happened, Han Li brought her left knee to her chest and extended her foot into the left passenger window at a speed approaching 125 mph, shattering the glass on impact. She leaned out the newly created opening and put her left hand through the driver's side window at a speed of 100 mph, pulverizing its glass into tiny fragments. Both actions happened so fast that Zika swerved to the side of the road and slammed on the brakes in a conditioned response that brought the car to a screeching halt.

As the vehicle came to a stop, Han Li reached out and opened her door. In little more than the time that it took to snap one's finger, she stepped outside the car and put her right fist into Zika's jaw. She then shifted her weight and, with Vallas looking at her, extended her right foot into his temple. Both men were out for the count.

When Zika and Vallas regained consciousness, they discovered their legs and hands were bound with zip ties, and they were hanging upside down 100 feet above the jagged rocks along the shore of the Aegean Sea. The rope from which they dangled, which Moretti found in the cruiser's trunk with the zip ties, was tied to the vehicle's bumper. As they struggled to get out of their bonds, Moretti and Han Li looked down at them.

"Here's the situation," Moretti said. "We're a mile off the main highway and in an area that, judging from the lack of footpaths or tire tracks, no one cares about. Someone sent you two scumbags to get Jehona. We want to know the name of that person and where we can find them."

Instead of answering, Zika responded with a threat that fellow officers knew they'd come to their hotel room to get the girl and that neither he nor "the bitch" with him would leave the country alive until they released him and his partner unharmed.

"Nice try. I don't think anyone in the police department knows that you came to our room or have knowledge of Jehona. Let's cut the bullshit. One last chance. Who sent you two, and where can we find them?"

"I'll slice your heart in half when I get out of this," Vallas said in response.

"Fair enough. We'll do this the hard way. I learned many interrogation techniques in the army. One of them is that if you hang someone upside down for prolonged periods of time, bad things happen. The liver and intestines, which should be below the lungs, are now above it. These organs are heavy. Your lungs are getting squished. That means your body isn't getting enough oxygen, and you'll eventually suffocate. Getting a little light-headed?"

Both men let out a string of obscenities. Moretti ignored them and continued explaining their predicament.

"The second problem is the pooling of blood in your brain. You should expect a ruptured blood vessel or brain hemorrhage."

The two men became silent.

"What I've told you so far are not your biggest problems. What will kill you first is that, as your hearts slow down because it's receiving more blood than it can pump, your blood pressure will decrease. When that happens, the blood can't get to every part of the body, and your organs deteriorate. You're dying as we speak."

The two men remained silent.

"I'm going back to the car and take a nap. When you two losers die, I'll cut your ropes and let you fall onto the rocks. The crabs that I see below will get rid of any trace of you."

Moretti and Han Li went back to the vehicle and sat beside Jehona for ten minutes, ignoring Zika and Vallas's pleading screams. When they returned to the edge of the cliff, both men said they were ready to talk.

"You're not going anywhere until one of you tells me who sent you and where I can find them," Moretti responded.

Both said Behar Tosku.

"Where can I find him?" Han Li asked.

"In a compound close to here. That's where we were taking you," Zika responded.

After answering several more questions, Moretti and Han Li pulled them onto the plateau and cut their ties. Even though the officers could now attack them, they looked at Han Li like the devil reincarnated and remained docile.

"Let's get back to Athens," Moretti said. "I'm going to put you both in the trunk of your vehicle. You can retell your story to an honest cop. Fair warning. If you suffer a memory lapse, I'll play this," Moretti said, taking his cell phone from his pocket and hitting the play function on his Recorder Plus app.

Zika and Vallas recoiled at the sound of their voices and what they disclosed.

"We won't be alive in the morning if you turn us in and play that. Let us go, and we'll leave Athens," Zika pleaded.

"A leopard doesn't change its spots. You'll find another scumbag to work for. Besides, child traffickers are the lowest forms of life, and I'm giving you a break by turning you in. If Jehona wasn't here, I'd toss you both to the crabs. Now, walk to the car and get in the trunk."

Although Moretti confiscated Zika and Vallas's handguns from their shoulder and ankle holsters and patted them down before cinching their zip ties, he didn't check Vallas's jacket lining. That was a mistake because a switchblade was cleverly concealed beneath the loosely stitched fabric. Moretti never saw him pull apart the stitching. If he hadn't moved to follow Han Li to the vehicle, the blade would have pierced his heart. Instead, it made a deep gash in his upper left torso.

What happened next took five seconds. Zika, standing behind Han Li and seeing what Vallas had done, grabbed her throat in both hands and squeezed. Having powerful hands, the dozen people he'd strangled in this manner for Tosku never lasted long before they suffocated. But none had Han Li's skills. Once his hands locked on her neck, she grabbed his right hand, found a pressure point, and pressed it so hard that the pain elicited a primal scream. He released his grip. She then slammed her fist into the left side of his chest with such force that it stopped his heart. Zika was dead before he hit the ground.

As this was happening, Moretti was fighting for his life. Despite a six-inch gash that was pouring blood, he grabbed Vallas's knife hand and, being stronger and sixty pounds heavier than his assailant, turned the tip of the blade towards him and thrust it into his left eye. Game over.

"It's deep, but it didn't nick an artery," Moretti said as Han Li ran over and examined the wound.

"You'll need some stitches. But that's a routine occurrence for you."

"It's funny how my scars started after I partnered with you. Cut a strip from Vallas's shirt so I can plug this wound."

Han Li pulled the knife from the detective's eye, cut off his shirt, and made a bandage for Moretti, which he pressed against the wound to stem the flow of blood until he could get it stitched.

As he got into the car's front passenger seat, Han Li dragged both bodies to the edge of the cliff and pushed them over.

Jehona was lying down in the back seat of the car when Moretti got in. Sitting up, she saw him compressing a blood-drenched shirt to his upper torso.

"I don't want to talk about it," Moretti said in response to the look he was receiving.

"They wanted to give me back to the men who took me," Jehona said. They deserved to die."

Moretti was surprised at her response. He got out of the car and waited for Han Li.

"She saw us kill the detectives but says they deserved to die because they were going to give her back to her abductors."

"Given all she's been through, she's grown up."

"Let's go back to Athens and find a police officer who isn't on Tosku's payroll so they can protect Jehona and arrange for her to return to the orphanage. They have to be worried about her."

Han Li said she agreed, and they got back into the vehicle and told Jehona what they were going to do. However, if they believed the diminutive person in the back seat would blindly go along and didn't have her own opinion, they were mistaken.

"We have to save the others. We can't abandon them," Jehona said in an unemotional and confident voice that appeared to have come from someone a decade older. "I don't have a family, but most of them do."

"She's right," Moretti said.

Han Li also agreed. "Any ideas?" she asked.

"Only that I should call Cray and tell him what's going on. Even though this doesn't concern Nemesis, it involves us. Afterward, we'll check out of the hotel and find somewhere safe to keep Jehona until we sort this out."

Cray answered his cell after the second ring and, looking at the screen, was surprised to find that Moretti was calling.

"If I were on vacation with someone as beautiful as Han Li, I wouldn't be wasting my time calling the office," Cray said before Moretti could utter a word.

"I don't disagree, but something's come up. We need to talk on an encrypted line. You never know what neighbors will be listening."

"Go to the US Embassy. I'll have the president send the ambassador a message telling him to expect the both of you."

"Three of us," Moretti corrected. "Add Jehona Dibra to the access list. By the way, she doesn't have an ID. Also, make sure they have someone there who can stitch me up."

"I can't wait to hear this story."

"You're not going to like it."

"On that, I expect we'll agree."

CHAPTER 3

I N ATHENS, THE US embassy compound stood out like a sore thumb in a city saturated with ancient historical buildings. Dominated by a white modernistic 50,000-square-foot structure said to be inspired by the Parthenon's architecture, only an enlightened few could make that comparison - most of whom were on the architect's payroll.

Han Li, getting directions from her cellphone, pulled the police cruiser to a screeching halt in front of the embassy's main entry gate. The two Greek police officers in tactical gear, who were there to keep unauthorized persons from getting into the compound, saw the vehicle with two shattered windows and turned off the safety on their automatic weapons - which prevented the trigger from engaging. In a loud voice that reflected their nervousness, they ordered everyone out of the cruiser in Greek and, when no one responded, in English.

As Moretti opened his door and stepped out, the guards saw the blood-soaked fabric pressed to his chest. Ordering the three in English to raise their hands, Moretti replied he couldn't comply because he was bleeding and needed to maintain pressure on his wound. That was as far as the discussion went as the US Ambassador to Greece, Kyle Pullen, approached the gate. He told the guards to lower their weapons in an urgent voice because the three people they were pointing their guns at were there by invitation. Accompanying the ambassador were three US Marines.

Pullen was six feet, two inches tall, with gray hair parted to the right. He had a thick chest and, judging from how his clothes fit, a muscular physique. Appearing to be in his mid to late 60s, he wore a navy-blue three-piece suit.

"Drive him to the infirmary, then park their vehicle out of sight in the garage," Pullen said, addressing two of the marines by name.

The Greek officers watched as one marine helped Moretti into the vehicle's rear before getting into the driver's seat. His partner sat beside him.

The infirmary wasn't large, but the doctor was first-rate, and Moretti added 20 stitches to his list of scars. Once the doctor finished, the marine escorted him to the ambassador's office where Han Li and Jehona were sitting with Pullen.

"The doctor told me you'll be ready for your next knife fight in no time."

Moretti laughed.

"This little lady has quite a story," Pullen said, as Moretti took a seat between Han Li and Jehona on the couch to the right of the brown overstuffed chair on which the ambassador was sitting. "President Ballinger asked me to help you both in any way I could, leaving the amount of cooperation up to me. He said that you'd protected our country and the world in ways that would forever go untold. He also said that you were an ex-Army Ranger, Mr. Moretti. That means I'm giving you a blank check. Just tell me what you need."

Moretti thanked him.

"No, thank you. Jehona told me you're trying to find who kidnapped and trafficked her. If it were up to me, I would put a bullet in the head of anyone involved in human trafficking."

"We have the name of the person behind this, but our priority is to rescue the others that he's enslaved," Moretti said.

"A question. Will the police officers who loaned you their vehicle be needing it back?"

"No, sir. They won't be needing anything from now on."

"Then I'll have one of the marines abandon it some distance from the embassy."

"I have to call my boss in Washington. Is it possible to use your secure line?"

"There's several, one of which is on my desk. There's another in a soundproofed room down the hall that will give you complete privacy. I'll take you there when you're ready."

"Since the person who we're after knows our hotel, we can't return to the Grande Bretagne. Any idea where we can stay that's below the radar of anyone searching for us?" Moretti asked.

"Here. The embassy is your home while in Athens. I'll send someone to get what you left in your hotel room."

"If you don't mind my saying, you're unlike any ambassador I've met. I mean that as a compliment."

"I'm an ex-Army Ranger myself, hoo-ah! I retired after putting in twenty and then got a cushy civilian job. I try to keep in shape, but age takes its toll. Just like you, I've seen my share of hell on earth. But here's the thing: I never shed a tear for the scum I've sent to the netherworld, and I won't for those that you and Ms. Li are going to dispatch to join them."

"How did you become an ambassador?" Han Li asked.

"President Ballinger and I are both from Salina, Kansas. I campaigned for him when he was running for Senate and then the presidency. When he asked me to accept this position to better the relationship between both countries, I couldn't say no. Now, let's get you to that secure phone."

Pullen led the way to the small office with the encrypted phone. Moretti spoke to Cray and filled him in. As expected, Cray said that Tosku's operations, no matter how heinous, were outside of Nemesis' mission parameters, and if he or Han Li were apprehended while doing something illegal in Greece or anywhere else, not to expect his help. "In Athens, you're tourists. Period," Cray said.

When Moretti returned to Pullen's office, Han Li asked how it went.

"We're on our own, as expected."

"Then it's up to us to rescue the trafficking victims. Where do we start?"

As it turned out, the answer to that question was obvious.

Defrim Kote was a colonel with the Hellenic Police. He had close-cropped black hair, was forty years old, five feet, ten inches in height, and was a muscular 170 pounds. The Athens native's reputation was one incorruptibility, which cemented his relationship with the US ambassador.

Over the years, he'd provided Pullen with intelligence on terror cells and extremists targeting American interests in the region. Although Kote could have acted against these groups, he let the Americans take the offensive and the credit without his superior's knowledge on the condition that his involvement remains secret. The reason for this decision, which he shared with Pullen, was that there were so many leaks within his department that it was the flip of a coin whether they would compromise an upcoming operation. The Americans neutralized terrorists quietly and efficiently. As tourism accounted for 20 percent of all jobs and was a significant component of the country's GDP, it was essential not to spook tourists.

Kote drove to the US embassy in the same make and model cruiser that Zika and Vallas had driven. Before his arrival, a marine drove the damaged vehicle to a remote part of the city and abandoned it with the keys in the ignition. Pullen told Moretti he'd thought about telling Kote about the altercation with two of his officers but kept it a secret as it would put them in a difficult position because of conflicting loyalties.

Pullen introduced Kote to Moretti and Han Li, saying that they worked for the president. This impressed the hell out of him. He then introduced Jehona. The ambassador then repeated the edited version of what Moretti told him.

"You said that three men attacked you a quarter of a mile from your hotel?" Kote asked Moretti, who nodded in agreement. "They'll still be looking for her. In the world of human trafficking, someone her age is worth a great deal of money."

"Do you have any idea who these men work for?"

"It's not a secret. His name is Behar Tosku. He lives in an immense mansion near Rafina, a small port town of about thirteen thousand that's a short distance from here."

Moretti didn't volunteer that he received the same information from one of the deceased officers, who was now a protein source for the crabs near Tosku's mansion.

"If you know he's a human trafficker, why not arrest him?" Han Li asked.

"Because knowing and proving are vastly different. Tosku acts through intermediaries. He doesn't use the internet nor has a cell phone. He gives his orders verbally. Therefore, it's challenging to prove his involvement in anything illegal-not that anyone would live long enough to testify against him. He owns many companies through offshore corporations-import and export, shipping, an inter-island airline-the list goes on and on. Because he employs many people and pays a tremendous amount in taxes, at least from his legal enterprises, the politicians have told us to stay away from him unless we have solid proof that he's involved in a crime."

"You described his legal enterprises," Han Li said. "What do you know about his illegal activities?"

"Rumors that he'll get someone whatever they want for a price."

"And that includes selling people," Han Li said.

"Especially human trafficking. Let me give you a few statistics from a report I received. Globally, there are 24.9 million victims of modern-day slavery. Human trafficking is estimated to generate $32 billion in profits per year. Two-thirds of this money comes from sexual exploitation; 20 percent from construction, mining, and other forms of manual labor; and the rest from agriculture, forestry, fishing, and other areas of labor too numerous to list."

"Two-thirds of the trafficker's victims are sexually exploited?" Moretti asked.

"Only 19 percent of the victims are trafficked for sex, but they generate two-thirds of the profits for these degenerates. For example, Jehona is worth $100,000 to Tosku because he expects someone her age to generate over $18,000 per month in profits."

"What about laborers?" Moretti asked.

"Indications are they sell for around $20,000, but the report indicates that a trafficker will take as little as $90 to get someone off their hands. Women and girls account for 55 percent of trafficked labor. One business owner purchased a laborer for his Chinese kitchen and paid her an average of $808 for a 78-hour workweek. Under Chinese law, she was entitled to $2,558 for a 39-hour workweek. The Asia-Pacific region accounts for 62 percent of forced laborers, while Europe and Central Asia is only nine percent."

"The report you referenced seems comprehensive," Han Li said.

"We've learned about trafficking over the years. We understand that 90 percent of trafficked victims come through Greece and go to other European Union countries. Ten percent remain in the country. Those within the department refer to victims of human trafficking as the forgotten because few are rescued."

"The forgotten," Pullen repeated. "Where do the forgotten come from?"

"Primarily Eastern Europe and the Balkans. Within those areas, the Ukrainians, Bulgarians, and Gypsies have the largest number of trafficked victims. However, being politically correct, I'll refer to the last group as Roma."

"If you can recall, give me some numbers," Pullen said.

"Over the last decade, 420,000 women, between the ages of 17 and 27, were trafficked from the Ukraine, and 10,000 a year from Bulgaria. It's hard to get statistics on the Roma ethnic group."

"Are most victims women and children?" Han Li asked.

"Yes. Eighty percent are women, and half are children. The average age of a child entering the sex trade is between 12 and 14."

"How many were rescued?" Han Li asked.

"Between one and two percent. However, those statistics are misleading because, in Eastern Europe, 80 percent of rescued women are re-trafficked, most within two years of their escape."

"How many of Tosku's are in jail for these horrific crimes?" Pullen asked.

"In the EU, only 1 in 100,000 of those involved in trafficking are convicted."

"And you're convinced Tosku is behind this?" Moretti asked. "His name doesn't sound Greek."

"He's Albanian by birth with dual citizenship in Greece. He doesn't travel much, fearing he'll be kidnapped or killed by the Mafia, Union Corse, or another rival."

"Any idea how we can take him into custody for questioning?" Han Li asked.

"Get the military to storm his compound. Short of that, you will not lay a hand on him. But you can put a gouge in his pocketbook. Thanks to this young lady," Kote said, looking at Jehona, "we may know the location of one of his trafficking houses. I know it's a lot to ask, but do you think you can bring us there?" Kote requested, looking at Jehona.

"Take me to where they rescued me, and I'll find the building I escaped from," Jehona replied.

After leaving the embassy, Kote stopped by his office and, bringing three trusted officers, met Moretti and Han Li at the site of their altercation with Tosku's men. Each of the officers carried an assault rifle and wore the same tactical gear that one might see on a SWAT team. The young girl unerringly led them down an alley through which she ran and to the place from which she'd escaped.

The entire area looked to have been constructed 50 years ago, with every building in need of some repair. The building from which Jehona bolted was a decrepit two-story structure at the end of a row of low-end residential units and retail shops. Its wooden facing had long ago warped, and the paint deteriorated so that its cracks resembled light gray reptilian skin. There were no windows on the bottom floor and only three on the second, all of which had black fabric curtains covering them. There was one entrance, and that door was made of steel.

"It looks like a drug house," Kote said.

"Or a prison," Moretti countered.

Kote told an officer to forget about knocking and blow the door off its three hinges. The officer placed plastic explosives at strategic points on the door and inserted the detonators. After confirming that everyone was clear, he pressed the red button on his remote transmitter. Simultaneous with a large booming sound, the door separated from its hinges and fell to the ground.

Neither Moretti nor Han Li was about to wait outside, even though neither had a weapon. Rushing into the building behind Kote and his men, they followed the team as it went from room to room. Seven minutes later, the search ended.

"The inside of this place is cleaner than my mother-in-law's apartment," Kote said.

"Bleach," Moretti volunteered as he sniffed the air. "That'll destroy even trace DNA."

"I'll have my officers ask the merchants in the area if they saw anything. Even if they did, they'd claim temporary blindness and deafness given that they almost certainly knew what was going on here."

"And being too curious or talking about what they saw would be bad for their longevity."

"Precisely."

"Any idea where the forgotten went since you're familiar with Tosku's tactics?" Han Li asked, using the same term for human trafficking victims as Kote.

"To another safe house in the city. He views people like Jehona as merchandise and will want to make them readily available to his customers."

Moretti and Han Li's look of disgust matched the expression on Kote's face.

Once outside, Han Li approached Jehona and told her that the building was empty. The look of disappointment on the young girl's face was gut-wrenching. "You'll keep looking?" she asked, the sound of her voice a combination of hope and desperation.

"You have my word."

"Back to square one," Moretti said as he watched Kote's men putting police tape around the building.

Once they returned to the embassy, Moretti and Han Li briefed the ambassador.

"You don't win wars in a day," Pullen said as he led them out of his office and into a conference room where an array of Greek foods and an assortment of beverages were on the table. "They're won over time by tenacity and persistence. I know little about either of you, but you both have these traits in spades from what I've been able to observe. Enjoy the meal and try to put some meat on this young lady's bones." Pullen left the room and closed the door behind him.

When Moretti and Han Li turned around, they saw Jehona's eyes locked on the feast in front of her. Han Li handed the skinny teenager a plate and told her to dig in. Once everyone had their fill, Han Li wanted to know more about what happened to Jehona.

"You told us earlier that they kidnapped you in your hometown of Tirana, Albania, and put you on two different boats to bring you to Athens."

The young girl confirmed that was true.

"Do you know the Albanian town where you boarded the first boat?" Han Li asked.

"Sarande."

Moretti and Han Li showed surprise, which produced a smile from the spirited teenager.

"I saw it painted on a sign at the dock."

"And do you know where you went from there?" Moretti asked.

"I overheard two of the guards talking. One said we were on our way to Nissaki. Later, a girl on the cot next to me said that was in Corfu."

"How long did you stay in Corfu?" Han Li asked.

"Two nights. The girl next to me said she'd been there for two weeks."

"Did they hide you on the boats?"

"Only on the one coming here."

"Where did they hide you?" Moretti asked.

"I don't know. I was blindfolded and taken down three ladders to a hot room with a lot of noisy equipment, where they pushed me through a hole that led into a large steel room. They took my blindfold off inside. The room smelled of oil. I threw up once because of it."

"That sounds like you were next to the engine room," Moretti said.

"What happened once they took you off the ship in Athens?" Han Li inquired.

"They put us in a van and drove us to the place I showed you."

"Blindfolded?"

"Yes."

Jehona was unemotional as she relayed her story. Han Li got up from the table and motioned for Moretti to join her out of earshot of the teenager.

"Seeing a lack of emotion when she's telling us what happened tells me she's no stranger to adversity because of the harsh life she lives. If they went to all this trouble getting her here, Tosku would keep coming after Jehona long after we're gone. We need to make sure that doesn't happen," Han Li said.

"You know what that means?"

"We kill Tosku, and every person involved in her kidnapping."

As fate would have it, they came incredibly close.

CHAPTER 4

THE PORT OF Rafina lies on the Aegean Sea. The facility has thirteen piers for docking ships and two areas where speedboats and other craft can tie-up. Along with Piraeus and Lavrio, it's one of the three ports that serve Athens and ferries disembark for the Greek islands.

It was after dark, and the docks showed no activity. Moretti, Han Li, and Jehona were on a hill overlooking them, waiting for a ship to enter the port and offload human cargo. They expected it would arrive at night, not only because Jehona said that's when she did, but because the traffickers could hardly herd a group of children into vans during daylight without attracting attention. The port was a beehive of activity during the day but the opposite at night.

Moretti and Han Li agreed Tosku's ships wouldn't arrive every day. Therefore, there was no telling how long they would have to surveil the port. Ambassador Pullen provided his full cooperation, letting them use one of the embassy's black Chevy Suburban's and handing them night vision binoculars. Although Jehona insisted on staying awake and helping with surveillance, Han Li was adamant that she remain in the vehicle and sleep. As with anything involving teenagers, there was a negotiation until they struck a deal. In return for her staying in the car, Han Li promised to wake Jehona if they discovered anything.

The first night was a bust, and so was the second. On the third, they saw what those in the port referred to as a handysize carrier pull into port - the term referring to a small freighter of between 10,000 - 30,000 DWT or deadweight tonnage - the measure of how much weight a ship can carry. The giveaway that this was the ship was when two windowless white vans pulled onto its dock just as it anchored. As promised, Han Li woke Jehona and told her what was happening. Five minutes later, a port authority vehicle pulled by one van, and two customs officers got out. The driver, rolling down his window, handed a fat envelope to each official, who then returned to their vehicle and left the area.

It wasn't long before a row of disheveled and blindfolded children was herded from the ship and into the vans.

"Time to follow them," Moretti said as he led the way back to their vehicle.

Once everyone was in the Suburban, he raced to the main roadway. Pulling the vehicle to the side and killing the headlights, everyone waited. Less than a minute later, the two windowless vans streaked past. Moretti turned on the Suburban's headlights and followed.

Entering Athens thirty minutes later, the vans pulled into the driveway of a decaying two-story house off Omonoia Square, a rough area known to be the center of the city's drug, prostitution, and contraband trade.

"It's hard to stay inconspicuous in a vehicle like this," Moretti said. "Everyone's trying to determine if we're law enforcement or someone who intends to encroach on their territory."

"I'll take a photo and get the coordinates of the house with my phone's GPS," Han Li responded.

Once she did, they returned to the embassy and entered the compound without incident, using the remote control in the Suburban to open the gates.

Jehona was asleep in the back of the vehicle, and Han Li woke her up and helped her inside the embassy and to her room, while Moretti called Pullen to see if he was working on US time. He was. Moretti went to his office to give him chapter and verse on what happened.

"What do you intend to do?" Pullen asked.

"Tell Colonel Kote and see if he can raid the house in Omonoia Square and impound the ship at the dock. That gets us one step closer to taking down Tosku."

"I'll call him in the morning." Pullen looked at his watch. "Correction, later this morning. Let's set the meeting for nine."

At nine, Moretti, Han Li, and Jehona went to the ambassador's office and found Colonel Defrim Kote seated beside Pullen, who looked rested despite getting only a few hours of sleep. In contrast, Moretti appeared to be sleep-deprived and had dark circles under his eyes. Following a cup of strong coffee that put caffeine into his system, he rapidly gained consciousness. He gave the colonel a detailed report on what happened at both the port and Omonoia Square, repeating what he told Pullen hours before. Kote listened without interruption, asking his first question once Moretti finished.

"Do you have the name of the ship and the address of the house?"

"The ship is the *Green Seas*," Han Li answered, following with the house's GPS coordinates. Kote wrote both on a notepad that he removed from his jacket pocket.

"Excuse me while I make a call," the colonel said to no one as he got up and walked to the back of the ambassador's office. A short time later, he returned to his chair.

"The *Green Seas* belongs to an Albanian shipping company that operates three other vessels - the *Green Harbor*, the *Green Island*, and the *Green Port*," Kote said, referencing his notepad. "The company is owned by an offshore trust, the beneficial owner of which we're unable to determine. This same trust owns the house."

"What's your next step?" Moretti asked.

"Rescue the children. I'll assemble a team, and we'll enter the house before the end of the day."

"Mind if we tag along?" Moretti asked the tentative look on his face showing that he didn't know what answer he'd receive.

"I'm grateful for your help. Without you, none of this would be happening. I'll let you know what time we'll breach the residence, then have one of my men pick you both up."

At five that evening, 20 men, handpicked by Kote, surrounded the decaying two-story house off Omonoia Square. Arriving in three unmarked vans and two police cruisers, the officers parked their vehicles in the center of the street. While one of them placed explosive charges on the steel door, seven officers established a perimeter around the house. Moments later, they blew the door from its hinges, and a dozen officers stormed inside. Six spread out on the first floor, and the remaining six went upstairs. The person who placed the explosive charges secured the entrance.

There were four bad guys inside the building, which Tosku considered more than enough to handle up to 40 scrawny and frightened children. Upon hearing the explosion, the two thugs on the first floor drew their weapons and ran towards the entrance, where they came face-to-face with the breaching team and took multiple bullets to the body. The two thugs on the second floor didn't fare any better. Both tried hiding behind young girls when the officers entered the room, which occupied the entire second floor. Much taller than the children, each took a single round in the face.

Once they secured the house, Moretti and Han Li, accompanied by Kote, entered. Looking upstairs, they saw four rows of cots, ten cots to a row, each covered with a filthy sheet and pillow. At the far end of the room was a single bathroom and shower. Children, some appearing to be as young as eight, were cowering next to their beds.

"I wish I could have been the one to put a round in their heads," Moretti said, looking at the two dead men.

"Tosku considers them expendable minions," the colonel said.

As they were speaking, a dozen medical professionals entered the large room, talked to the children, and began examining them.

"Any idea how we can link Tosku to this?" Han Li asked Kote.

"None, I'm sorry to say."

"What now?" Moretti asked.

"Since the children arrived on The *Green Seas*, I'm going to impound the ship and start the paperwork to have it auctioned. I'll do the same with this house. Neither will be financially significant to Tosku. The real impact won't be monetary; it'll be to his reputation. If his competitors sense he's vulnerable, they'll go after his customers and encroach on his territory."

"How do you think he'll respond?" Han Li asked.

"Like most psychopaths, he has a temper and responds quickly and violently. We'll know what form that takes soon enough."

And they did.

The news of losing thirty-five children and his ship reached Tosku within an hour of the raid, thanks to a call from several paid informants within the Athens police department. The forty-one-year-old billionaire took the mug of coffee he was holding and flung it across the room, barely missing Gashi as it streaked past him and impacted his office wall.

"Colonel Kote, the American ambassador, and the two foreigners have not only cost me millions today, but their actions have forced me to renegotiate with my buyers to provide suitable substitutes. Do you realize how demeaning that is?"

"What do you want me to do?"

"Kill them."

"If we kill the ambassador, and the Americans discover we're behind it, they'll come after us."

"Make it look like a terrorist attack. Someone is always trying to kill American diplomats. Get the job done."

"There will be collateral damage."

"There's always collateral damage in terrorist attacks. I don't care if you take out a city block."

"What about the girl?"

"Kill her and photograph the body. I want the others to understand that, even if they escape, I'll find them."

CHAPTER 5

IDING IN THE bushes, Gashi waited for Kote to exit the parking lot beneath the police headquarters building, the sixteen-story concrete and glass structure across the street from him. Talking to an informant, he learned the colonel was a creature of habit and that, barring something unforeseen, he arrived at his office between 8:30 a.m. and 9 a.m. and left between 7:00 p.m. to 7:30 p.m. It was now 7:15 p.m. The informant also provided the make, model, and license plate number of his police cruiser. Gashi was sweating, and his heart was beating with excitement anticipating the kill. Thankfully, the exit to the parking lot was well lit and less than 50 yards away, which allowed him to see the drivers' faces. This was important since Kote was in an unmarked police cruiser that looked the same as every other unmarked law enforcement vehicle except for the license plate.

Gashi adjusted the 15 pound and 37 inches long Type 69 85mm rocket-propelled grenade tube that sat on his right shoulder. The weapon was too heavy to lift at a moment's notice. Therefore, he kept it on his shoulder and ready to fire. As he adjusted the RPG, he saw a white 2007 Toyota Aygo police cruiser exit the garage. The license plate number matched Kote's. A moment later, his target's face became visible. Gashi leveled the RPG, locked the sight on the front grill of the Toyota, and pressed the trigger. Instantly, a propellant exploded and drove the 5.7-pound high-explosive grenade from the launcher at 384 feet per second. The grenade, which could penetrate between 19 and 29 inches of Rolled Homogenous Armor, the protective covering for tanks and armored vehicles, penetrated the thin-skinned Toyota Aygo grill like it was nonexistent. The impact crushed a piezoelectric fuse at the tip of the RPG and created a small electrical current that triggered the shaped charge within the projectile. An instant later, the vehicle became shrapnel. The colonel, in the center of the grenade's 40-foot kill radius, died instantly.

Wiping his prints from the launcher, Gashi left it in the bushes and returned to his car. His next target would be the United States embassy.

Gashi's plan for killing the US ambassador, Moretti, Han Li, and the girl depended on destroying the American embassy. He'd pin the attack on terrorists, telling the police detectives and government officials on Tosku's payroll who did it.

The choice of weapon was critical for assigning blame, as every terrorist group had its favorite weapons. Fortunately, he knew who to blame and what weapon he needed to implicate them. He selected the Serbian Advanced Light Attack System, or ALAS - guided to its target by a fiber-optic cable that connected the missile to the launcher. Tosku sold these to half a dozen terrorist organizations. It had a 15-mile range and was used to destroy industrial facilities and hardened targets. It was the perfect choice to demolish the targeted structures within the embassy compound.

While Gashi was busy setting up his ambush, Tosku's weapons experts went to his warehouse. They programmed the two ALAS missiles he had in inventory, entering the geographic coordinates of the targets within the embassy and the route each would take to get there before bringing them to the launch site. Each 132-pound missile, which was slightly longer than eight-feet, was within an olive-green launch tube affixed to the bed of a short twin axle flatbed truck. Both missiles were on the same vehicle. Since going through the streets of Athens with two missile launchers would generate more than a few phone calls to law enforcement, they hid them beneath a thick canvas tarp. In appearance, the flatbed was one of many transporting merchandise within the city.

When Gashi arrived at a secluded part of an athletic field ten miles from the embassy, the missiles were ready for launch. All one needed to do was flip up the plastic safety covers and press the red buttons. Wasting no time, that's what he did. Those actions ignited a turbojet engine within each ALAS and propelled them along their programmed courses. One minute and thirty-six seconds later, they impacted the embassy compound.

The first ALAS hit the modern glass-fronted embassy building, transforming it into rubble. If there was any, the good news was that it was nighttime, and the building was largely unoccupied. However, the bad news was that there were six embassy employees inside. All died without realizing what happened. The second missile took out a newly completed office building, the historic chancery building, the parking garage, and the fuel station. When the fuel station ignited, the secondary explosion destroyed the swimming pool, basketball court, and the street park in front of the embassy.

Ten embassy personnel died in that explosion. Left standing were the Marine Corps barracks, quarters for civilians who lived in the embassy, and the ambassador's quarters.

At the moment of impact Moretti, Han Li, Ambassador Pullen, and Jehona were having a late dinner in the ambassador's private dining room next to his quarters. The concussion from the blast tossed everyone onto the floor, and glass flew from the windows and showered the room. Several minutes later, a marine rushed inside.

"What happened, sergeant?" Pullen asked, getting up from the floor. Moretti, Han Li, and Jehona were also getting to their feet. Everyone was unharmed.

"It appears to be a missile attack that destroyed several buildings within the compound."

"Get a rescue detail organized."

"I'm on it," the marine responded as he ran from the room.

Pullen called the US Secretary of State and the Greek Foreign Minister. Afterward, he walked to where Moretti, Han Li, and Jehona were standing.

"I'm seriously pissed off," Pullen said in a menacing tone.

"Tosku?" Moretti asked.

"That's my vote since he's an arms dealer, and you put a dent in his operation."

Pullen's phone rang. Seeing it was Greece's president, he went to the far corner of the room to have some privacy. Their conversation lasted fifteen minutes, during which the expression on the ambassador's face transitioned from one of concern to one reflecting a great deal of pain.

When the call ended, he took a deep breath, rubbed his eyes, and picked up the bottle of Basil Hayden 10-Year-Old Bourbon Whiskey that fell from his liquor cabinet onto the floor. He poured two fingers of the high rye content bourbon in three plastic cups that he retrieved from an adjacent bathroom and handed a cup to Moretti and Han Li. Not forgetting Jehona, he set his cup down, lifted the mini-fridge upright, removed a can of coke, and handed it to her.

"The president of Greece told me that the assault on the embassy was the second terrorist attack this evening," Pullen said, picking up his drink. "The first was outside police headquarters where someone sent an RPG into Defrim Kote's vehicle." Pullen downed the bourbon in several gulps. Moretti, who was a reformed alcoholic, handed his to the ambassador.

"AA," Moretti said to Pullen, referring to Alcoholics Anonymous.

"Good choice. Recently, I poured Defrim a drink from this very bottle. I'm going to miss him."

Moretti and Han Li were silent as Pullen downed Moretti's drink, and Han Li handed him hers.

"The Secretary of State told me that, just minutes after the attack, an Islamic group claimed responsibility. That, of course, is bullshit and Tosku's way of covering his tracks so that the US doesn't send a special forces team to pay him a visit in the middle of the night."

"You know little about Han Li and me," Moretti said, "but they're not the only ones who make house calls. We've been uninvited guests frequently."

"Let's talk," Pullen said.

Tosku listened as one of his informants, a high-level official in the Greek government, told him that the ambassador, Moretti, Han Li, and Jehona were alive. Hearing this, he let out a stream of expletives and ended the call.

Tosku understood he didn't have the firepower to level the entire embassy compound. With only two ALAS missiles in inventory, he could only choose two targets. The operations buildings were the logical choices, with the ambassador's office in one and the embassy's administrative functions in the other. That the attack would occur in the evening didn't matter because several of his sources said Pullen always worked late and went between both buildings as he coordinated with his staff. Therefore, Tosku believed the ambassador would be in one of those buildings. He also expected Moretti, Han Li, and Jehona to be near him since a source said that they usually were. Therefore, he never expected all four targets to survive.

"It's better we forget about them," Gashi said. "They know nothing about our operations. The Americans will believe this was a terrorist attack. If we go after the ambassador or the others again, they'll intensify their investigation, and who knows what they'll find out."

"No one hurts my business and lives to talk about it. And, if I don't respond and put their heads on pikes, my competitors will believe I'm vulnerable."

"Perhaps I can suggest another approach," Gashi said, explaining what he meant.

Tosku liked what he heard.

The messengered letter from the Athens Police Department, which was on their stationery, thanked the ambassador, Matt Moretti, and Han Li for rescuing Jehona Dibra. It indicated that the police department contacted an orphanage in Tirana, Albania, and verified Jehona was missing from there. To expedite her return, the Albanian government sent a plane and a representative who would accompany the orphan. The letter went on to say that the Albanian government invited Moretti and Han Li to be the guests of honor at a small ceremony when they arrive in Tirana. It concluded by stating the plane would depart at 3:00 p.m., which was an hour away, and that the aircraft was in a government hangar at the Athens International Airport.

Upon reading the letter, Pullen verified its authenticity by calling the police department and speaking with the captain who'd sent it.

"It sounds like this little lady is going home," Pullen said once he finished the call, handing the letter to Moretti, who shared it with Han Li.

Jehona looked sad, not overjoyed at the prospect of returning to Tirana.

"What's the matter?" Han Li asked.

"I don't want to go back to the orphanage. I want to stay with you."

"I know it's going to be difficult, but I promise that this won't be the last time you'll see us. You can FaceTime as often as you like. We'll always be your friends. We can't be your parents."

"I know. I was hoping."

That response forced Han Li to take a deep breath.

"We'd better get going," Moretti said to Pullen.

The ambassador called and ordered one of the newly rented embassy vehicles to the main gate. Ten minutes later, Moretti, Han Li, and Jehona were on their way to the airport.

They arrived outside the airport hangar at precisely 3 p.m. Waiting for them were two members of the Athens Police Department, one of whom was the captain who spoke with Pullen. Beside them was a six feet, two inches tall, distinguished-looking man in his mid-50s. He wore a conservative three-piece suit, white shirt, and blue-striped tie. His hair was gray and parted to the left. The rimless glasses he wore were too small for his enormous face and looked out of place. The credentials that he presented gave his name as Taulant Manjani, an official of the Albanian government.

After witnessing the showing of IDs, the embassy's Marine Corps driver left. As he was departing, Manjani opened the door into the hangar and closed it behind him after escorting everyone inside. Afterward, everything happened in a choreographed chain of events. The captain and the officer with him tased Moretti and Han Li with stun guns that they removed from their pockets. Concurrently, the fraudulent Albanian government official, Tosku's interrogator, stepped behind Jehona and pressed a chloroform-soaked rag over her nose while clasping his hand over her mouth. After the girl collapsed into unconsciousness, he returned the rag to the plastic bag he'd taken from his pocket.

As a Taser's effects last less than thirty seconds, the police officers quickly bound Moretti and Han Li's arms and legs with zip ties and placed a gag over their mouths. The three unconscious victims were then dragged to a corner of the hangar and thrown in the back of a windowless van.

When Moretti awoke, he found that his legs and wrists were bound and that someone gagged him. Wiggling into a sitting position against the steel wall behind him, he saw that Han Li was similarly restrained and was ten feet to his left. Jehona was beside her and was neither bound nor gagged. She had her legs drawn up to her chest and was shaking like a leaf.

The room they were in matched the description that the orphan gave of the secret ship enclosure in which they hid her and the other children on their journey to Athens. Likewise, they could smell oil permeating the air and hear the ship's engines. However, she failed to mention the camera affixed to the ceiling.

Thirty minutes later, Gashi opened the steel hatch and entered the enclosure. Behind him were three huge men, one of whom was carrying an automatic rifle. Jehona recoiled upon seeing them.

"I have someone who wants to meet the three of you," Gashi said, pulling Jehona off the floor and leading her out of the room. Two of the huge men cut Moretti and Han Li's leg ties and jerked them to their feet while the third kept his automatic rifle pointed in their direction. Gashi led the way across the engine compartment to a small conference room at the ship's bow. The three hostages sat in dirty rust-encrusted chairs in front of a deteriorating steel table, all secured to the steel flooring.

Standing at the back of the twenty-by-twenty-foot room was a handsome six-foot, one-inch-tall man.

"Remove their gags," Tosku said in his steely voice.

Once that occurred, he approached the table.

"If you're wondering why I didn't kill you in the hangar," he said, sitting in a chair at the head of the eight-seat rectangular table on which someone placed a clean cushion, "it's for two reasons. I need to discover what the three of you know about my operations and who you told. Since trust isn't a word in my vocabulary, when this ship docks, I have someone who's going to find out. He can be very persuasive. I also want to make a video of your gruesome deaths to discourage anyone else from trying to escape or interfering with my businesses."

"You dress impeccably, trying to epitomize culture and refinement. But you can't make a silk purse out of a sow's ear. Every human trafficker is a dirtbag and a piece of excrement,"

Moretti said, just before one of Tosku's men stepped forward and punched him on the right side of his face. Moretti shook it off and stared defiantly at Tosku.

"Look at her," Tosku said in an irritable voice, pointing at Jehona. "She's going to a client who will feed and clothe her better than she's accustomed. I've upgraded her life."

"Lucky her. Why don't you take her place? I'm sure your client must have a subservience training program."

Tosku nodded to the man behind Moretti. An instant later, his fist again found the side of Moretti's face, which was now swollen and bruised. The ex-Army ranger again shook it off.

"Tell Dumbo he should take off his silk panties. He hits like a girl."

That response got him another fist to the jaw and elicited a smile from Dumbo.

"A deficiency in manners is a trait of the intellectually inferior. As interesting as this conversation has been, I have a helicopter on deck that's waiting to take me to my compound, where my chef will prepare a thick Wagyu steak for dinner. While I'm enjoying my meal, the three of you will undergo a very unpleasant interrogation followed by a horrible death. I want you to remember something as you're dying," Tosku said, getting up from his chair, approaching Moretti, and bringing his face an inch for his. "You three are nothing more than chattel - insignificant and expendable."

CHAPTER 6

P RESIDENT BALLINGER WAS a two-term governor and one-term senator from Kansas before ascending to the nation's highest office. As a Midwesterner, he shared the Kansas traits of being friendly, polite, never acting rashly, and giving people the benefit of the doubt. However, after seeing photos of the embassy employees' mangled bodies, the chief executive was ready to adopt a lifelong New Yorker's traits. Ambassador Pullen's report indicated he believed a human trafficker and arms dealer named Behar Tosku was behind the attack. Further angering the president was a video from a Sentinel drone showing the kidnapping of Moretti, Han Li, and a young girl. At this moment, he wanted nothing more than to kill the son of a bitch and the accomplices responsible for these atrocities.

President Ballinger brought President Liu of China up to speed since Han Li and Moretti were members of Nemesis.

"Fortunately, you sent the stealth drone to survey the damage to the embassy," Liu said. "Otherwise, we'd never know about the kidnapping."

"The credit belongs to Major Daller, the drone's pilot." When he finished photographing the compound, the president explained that he saw Moretti, Han Li, and a young girl getting into an SUV and followed it to an airport hangar - wondering what they were up to and staying close in case they needed his help.

"That was a smart move, considering their history of getting into and out of situations most people wouldn't survive," President Liu said.

"Although the Sentinel didn't capture the actual abduction, it did record that they entered the hangar. However, when the doors opened, and the white van left, the hangar inside was empty. He assumed they were in the van."

The president explained that Daller followed the van to the port of Rafina, where he recorded Moretti, Han Li, and the girl taken from it onto a ship named the *Green Harbor*, which was now in the Adriatic Sea.

"How do we rescue them?" Liu asked. "I'd prefer not to use Nemesis. If anything went wrong, it would not only destroy both our country's relationship with the Greek government but also expose our off-the-books organization."

"There's another option," Ballinger said and explained what he had in mind.

Secretary of Defense Rosen was sitting in a room of pencil pushers, although they wore either an eagle or one or more star on their uniform. All were trying to figure out how one plus one equals three - which made no sense to anyone with a knowledge of accounting but did if one worked for the government. With a budget of almost $700 billion, all but $8 billion discretionary, and an expected budget in the next fiscal year of $718 billion, most would believe that the Department of Defense was rolling in cash. However, that was far from the truth. The DOD was so massive that no one, including the Secretary of Defense, could accurately predict the behemoth department's cash needs. One reason for this, among many, was that the military was always involved in conflicts - both on and off-the-books. Therefore, budgeting was usually a guesstimate, and the DOD was always looking for more money in response to the next unanticipated sucking sound.

Rosen came closer than any of his predecessors to understanding the department's cash needs. However, after eight hours of pouring through spreadsheet after spreadsheet and refusing to kick the can down the road, he couldn't find the cash he needed. Since he only had another day to submit his budget, everyone in the room would pull an all-nighter to determine who would have to do with less.

He was currently looking at the consequences of the sins of the past, where his predecessors robbed Peter to pay Paul. That created shortages, particularly in maintenance, where there were insufficient inventory parts to repair operational equipment, including aircraft. In the middle of trying to untangle this Gordian knot, he received a call from President Ballinger. He took it in his office.

The president got straight to the point and told the Secretary of Defense what he needed and that this was strictly between them. He also said that he wasn't to discuss or write a report on what they would discuss. Rosen was well-accustomed to operational secrecy and told him that their conversation and its consequences never occurred. The president then explained what he wanted.

Accessing his computer, Rosen found the real-time display for his forces' positions and determined that what POTUS requested was possible. He then informed the president that he could make it happen.

Since both men understood that nothing in Washington was free, even if the request came from POTUS, it did not surprise the president when the SecDef asked for something in return. Ballinger agreed, and the call ended. Rosen pressed a button on his desk phone, and the Secretary of the Navy came on the line. SecDef then issued a series of verbal orders, never mentioning the president's name. All that mattered to the person receiving those orders was that it came from someone higher in authority. Since it did, everyone down the food chain would receive the same directives, the expectation being that they would flawlessly execute whatever part of the operation given them.

Following his call with the Secretary of the Navy, Rosen returned to the conference room where he could hear the conversation still revolved around how to get an additional wad of cash for the maintenance of military hardware.

"I just spoke with the president," Rosen said, interrupting the discourse. "We're going to get a substantial bump in our black budget that will not only cover our shortfall but also give us some breathing room for unforeseen events."

"How big is that number?" one of the generals asked.

Rosen told him, rendering every person at the table speechless.

"Put a ribbon on this budget and get it submitted. I'll coordinate the transfer of funds with the president. Now, let's go back to the business of defending this great nation."

The USS *Marco Island* was an 842-foot-long amphibious assault ship with a displacement of 44,971 tons. Besides MV-22 Ospreys and various attack helicopters, it carried the Navy's newest and most sophisticated aircraft, the F-35B Lightning II fighter. The ship was returning to its homeport of Naples, Italy, from a visit to Split, Croatia, where it was the centerpiece of a US effort to improve cooperation between both nations' navies. Onboard for the journey was an eight-man squad from SEAL Team 4, based at the Naval Amphibious Base Little Creek in Virginia Beach, Virginia. The SEALs were a last-minute addition meant to impress the Croatian military brass, and they did.

Captain Charles Ruebensaal was on the bridge when the communications officer handed him a Flash Override message, a priority he hadn't before received in his 22 years in the Navy. Reserved for the National Command Authority, of which the President was the senior member, a message with this designation had precedence over all other traffic. After reading the orders, Ruebensaal phoned the officer in charge of the combat information center, located a deck below the bridge. The CIC was the vessel's tactical center that provided processed information for command and control within the ship's area of operation.

"I need you to link with a Sentinel drone that's in the area so we can receive its data and digital images. Is that possible?" Ruebensaal asked.

Told that it was, the captain gave him the Sentinel's frequency and technical data contained in the message. The officer in charge established the link in short order.

Acting on the next part of his message, Ruebensaal directed the helmsman, who was on the bridge and charged with steering the vessel, to set an intercept course for a ship in the Adriatic Sea, giving her the other vessel's speed and heading. The helmsman did her calculation, saying they were 52 minutes from intercept at flank speed and longer if they remained standard. The captain ordered an increase in speed.

Going to his sea cabin, which was just off the bridge, Ruebensaal summoned his executive officer and the SEAL team's commander and squad leader.

Lieutenant Eric Hunter, who the team called LT, pronouncing each letter separately, and Petty Officer First Class Nathan Frye entered the cabin just behind Commander Mack Kullman, the ship's executive officer. Hunter was five feet, ten inches tall, clean-shaven, weighed 170 pounds, and had brown hair and matching eyes. In his late 20s, his upper body was V-shaped and muscular. Frye was in his early 30s, had a similar build, but was one inch shorter and ten pounds lighter. He had blonde hair and gray eyes, with small amounts of yellow and brown in the iris. He was also clean-shaven. Kullman was five feet, eleven inches tall with sandy hair, blue-green eyes, and a thin muscular physique. An ex-Notre Dame punter, he was more a listener than a talker.

Although Ruebensaal was taller than the two SEALs, there was nothing V-shaped or muscular about him. He stood six feet, four inches tall, and weighed 200 pounds. His thinning black hair, which seemed likely to abandon him in a few years, stood in stark contrast to his bushy eyebrows.

The captain handed everyone a copy of the flash override message he'd received, then gave everyone a chance to read it. Once they did, he asked Hunter what support he required, telling him they were approximately 45 minutes from the intercept. "Does that give you enough prep time? If not, I can slow the ship down," Ruebensaal said.

"That's 40 minutes more time than my team needs."

"Do we know how many people are onboard the *Green Harbor* and how many of those are non-combatants?" Frye asked.

"Assume that everyone except the three you're going to rescue is a bad guy," Ruebensaal said.

"Air support?"

"I'll have AH-1Z vipers on alert for combat air support and a UH-1Y Venom to transport the non-combatants off the ship."

"Unfortunately, the only way to get you there without being detected is on a RIB," Kullman added, referring to a rigid inflatable boat. "Our combat helicopters are noisy, and they'll announce your arrival. However, using the RIB will mean a vertical climb from the waterline to the deck of the ship with, what I'm assuming, will be a heavy backpack."

"We train for this type of climb. It won't be a problem," Hunter responded.

"I heard they tell you in training that the only easy day was yesterday."

"They were right."

Twenty-five minutes later, when the *Marco Island* was within fifteen minutes of its target vessel, the captain ordered general quarters - a signal to the crew to prepare for battle or imminent damage. As the ship slowed, the SEAL team drove the RIB into the water and sped away. It was 1:00 a.m.

The RIB had a tough time intercepting the target vessel. Frye felt he was riding the prize bull at a rodeo as he fought to pull the craft parallel to the handysize cargo carrier. Getting in sync with the six to eight-foot waves and strong winds, he finally got the RIB alongside it. Holding it there, however, was proving difficult.

"Shoot," Hunter said into his mic, ordering the team member with the compressed air launcher to press the trigger. He did.

The launcher made a thumping sound, inaudible in the heavy wind, and expelled a rope ladder with grappling hooks up and over the ship's railing. The team member pulled hard on the end of the ladder, and the hooks took hold against the rail. Petty Officer Third Class Steve Kirk stepped forward and started his climb. As he did, a burning cigarette butt darted over his head. They had company.

Liridon Cano didn't have good eyesight, which was evident to anyone who saw that the lenses on his glasses were so thick one could use them for coasters. The Albanian was one of three *Green Harbor* maintenance men responsible for cleaning everything from its bathrooms to its decks. Although it wasn't a glamorous job by any stretch of the imagination, he was paid well - not only for his work but also to keep his mouth shut.

Tonight, he was having trouble sleeping., which wasn't unusual since he was an insomniac. Rather than lay in bed and stare at the bottom of the bunk above him, he came on deck. He was standing behind the railing, cupping his hand around his cigarette to keep it alive, when he heard the clang of steel hitting steel followed by a scraping sound. Cano flipped his cigarette into the wind, which carried it out to sea. Looking around, he saw a grappling hook ten feet to his right. Believing that pirates were attempting to board the vessel, he began yelling. No one heard him until he ran below deck and got the attention of his crewmates, one of whom called the bridge and said they were under attack by pirates - because that's what Cano told him. Not that it mattered to the captain. He had uninvited guests.

"Shut that guy up," Hunter said into his mic, clearly telling Kirk that as soon as he came over the railing to put a bullet in whoever was yelling.

However, by that time, Cano was below decks trying to wake his crewmates.

"There's no one around," Kirk replied. "He's probably gone to get help."

"Our presence won't be a secret for long," Hunter added.

His words proved prophetic because no sooner did the last set of boots come over the railing than the ship's lights came on, illuminating the deck as brightly as if they were standing in the noonday sun.

"The only thing missing to announce our arrival is a fucking band," Hunter said.

Dividing his team, he and two squad members went to the bridge to take control of the ship while the rest of his team would search below decks for the hostages. Frye was in charge of that group, directing half to descend the bow stairway and the other the stern. This way, they'd not only halve their search time but also pincer the bad guys between them.

That happened, discovering in the process the crew was well-armed and kicking the shit out of them - at least temporarily. Frye and Kirk were together at the ship's bow and got only three feet from the down stairway before a stream of bullets from automatic weapons started flying around them. Scrambling back to the stairway, which had a solid steel backing, they took cover behind it. They didn't know how many men were firing at them, but estimating that number from the rounds impacting the stairway, Frye believed it to be ten. Regardless, the ordinance coming in their direction was enough to blow an arm off if they reached from behind their cover and tried to return fire. Thankfully, those firing at them weren't military geniuses and didn't figure out that they could have their kills if they walked towards their targets as they fired.

"If they have nothing stronger than a bullet to throw at us, we can turn this around," Frye said to Kirk. "They've got to be grouped fairly close together. Take a baseball and see if you can flick it down the passageway without getting your fingers blown off."

Kirk removed an M67 fragmentation grenade from his tactical vest. Operatives called it a baseball because of its round shape. It had a safety delay of five seconds once the safety pin was pulled, and the spoon released the spring-loaded striker. When it exploded, steel fragments from the shattered grenade body produced a lethal radius of 16 feet and an injury radius of 49. Kirk didn't look where he tossed the grenade because he wanted to stay alive. Taking Frye's suggestion, he flicked it with as much force as he could down the passageway. The explosion was loud, and Frye and Kirk could hear the shrapnel hitting the stairway in front of them. Immediately thereafter, the gunfire was replaced with groans of agony. Cautiously stepping away from their cover, they saw ten men bunched together in the passageway. Five were dead and five wounded. Seconds later, they heard a similar explosion coming from the stern.

When Frye's men rendezvoused with the other group in a decaying conference room at the bottom of the vessel, a dozen wounded and shaken crew members sat in the rusted chairs or were lying on the deck. Eight crewmen lay where they fell and would require body bags.

Hunter had just as challenging a time getting to the bridge. He and the two men with him were pinned down behind a steel bulkhead, a hail of gunfire coming at them from two slimeballs standing on the platform atop the single ladder leading to the bridge.

"I'm not taking this shit any longer," Hunter said.

"Tiffany?" one of his men asked.

"Tiffany," Hunter confirmed as he removed an M203 from his backpack. The single-shot 40mm under-barrel grenade launcher was effective against exactly the resistance they were encountering. Everyone on the team knew Hunter named this weapon after a woman he dated in college who, he said, had skills he admired but were better left off her resume. As Hunter attached Tiffany to his M-4 assault rifle, Frye gave him an update through his earpiece.

"The ship is secure except for the bridge. Do you want help?"

"No, find the hostages. I don't know how much time we have if someone called for help. We'll be on the bridge in a few," Hunter said.

"Understood."

Loading an M576 buckshot round - a multipurpose projectile containing 20 steel pellets that escaped the launcher at a velocity of 882 feet per second, Hunter stuck Tiffany out from the corner of the bulkhead, pointed it in the general direction of his assailants, and pressed the trigger. The resulting explosion, which echoed around them, was so loud that it temporarily deafened the three men. Stepping from behind the bulkhead, they saw the lifeless bodies of two bad guys at the top of the ladder leading to the bridge.

Pushing the bodies aside, Hunter and the two team members with him entered the bridge to find the ship's captain spread-eagled on the deck. Starting to regain his hearing, Hunter pulled the power levers on the ship's control panel to stop, then ordered one of his men to secure the captain.

"We've taken the bridge," Hunter confirmed to Frye. "One prisoner and two who will need body bags. Did you find the hostages?"

"Negative."

"Let's assume the captain called for help. Seeing the resistance we encountered, I'm also assuming that whoever owns this rust bucket has the resources and motivation to send others. We need to leave with the hostages as quickly as possible. Grab someone and make them talk. This is a small ship. Everyone in the crew probably knows where they are."

"Roger that."

Selecting a prisoner at random, Frye grabbed the person wearing a thick pair of glasses. Dragging Liridon Cano into an adjoining room without saying a word, he tied his arms and legs to a chair while another team member guarded the door. Drawing three stick people on a sheet of paper - a man, woman, and child he asked in English where they were. The man wouldn't look at the drawing. Instead, Cano turned his head to the side and spit. Even though he might not speak English, Frye believed the man knew what he was after and avoided looking at his drawing. He was about to find out.

"I haven't got time for this," Frye said, striding to the back of what turned out to be a utility break room. Grabbing a case of bottled water and a large bowl, he put them on the table next to his prisoner and filled the bowl with water. Waterboarding is considered torture. All Frye knew was that it worked. After only one drenching, Cano led them to the hostages.

However, if Hunter thought he could now get off the ship or that his day would take a turn for the better, the call from Ruebensaal proved him wrong.

CHAPTER 7

THE CALL FROM Ruebensaal informed Hunter that the Sentinel drone spotted two Russian Mi-24 Hind helicopters streaking towards the *Green Harbor* at nearly 200 mph.

"How far away are the Hinds?" Hunter asked.

"Six miles. Your team and the hostages need to get off that ship now because each of those helicopters is carrying 12 Ataka missiles - more than enough to sink the *Green Harbor*."

"Can the *Marco Island* counter that threat?"

"I've ordered the launch of the Viper and Venom helicopters. But by the time they're airborne, the Hinds will be within five miles of the ship. That's within the range of their missiles."

"Options?"

"One. Get everyone into the RIB as fast as possible."

"I'm on it."

As Hunter ended the call, he heard Frye's voice in his in-ear conduction headset. "The three hostages are secure and mobile."

"Get them, yourself, and the team in the RIB now and cast off. Two Hinds are heading towards the ship with the probable intent of sinking it."

"What about you?"

"I have a dozen bound crewmembers on the main deck to cut loose so they can get off the ship and swim for it. Get to the RIB. That's an order."

"Roger that," was the unenthusiastic response.

Hunter, who was on the main deck, ran to the locker with a stencil of a lifejacket on the side. Opening it, he removed the lifejackets and put one in the lap of each of the crew. Withdrawing his knife, he cut the first crewman free and motioned for him to put on the lifejacket and jump off the ship. The man didn't move. When Hunter withdrew his gun and aimed it at his face, he got the point, putting on his lifejacket and leaping into the water. That process took thirty seconds. If Ruebensaal's timing was correct, he needed to speed it up. Frye arrived.

"I thought I ordered you into the RIB."

"You did, but I didn't want you to be the only one to receive a Purple Heart plus whatever medal they decide to throw in our coffins. Kirk cast off for the *Marco Island* with the rest of the team and the three hostages. Let's cut them loose and get them off the ship."

"Thanks, Nate," Hunter said. With both men cutting ties, the ship's crew were soon in the water, leaving them as the only two onboard.

"Time to get wet," Frye said.

"Too late," Hunter replied, pointing over Frye's shoulder to the pencil-thin smoke trails heading for the *Green Harbor*. Neither man moved, realizing that diving into the water wouldn't help because the missiles heading towards them would blow up the ship before they could get far enough away to either survive the explosion or be dragged under by the pull created by the vessel as it headed for the bottom.

Either way, they were dead. Frye gave the incoming missiles the finger in an ultimate act of defiance, an action quickly duplicated by Hunter.

Everyone in the RIB turned when they heard multiple explosions behind them, seeing oblong bursts of burnt orange in the distance. No one said a word, realizing the ship exploded and that Hunter and Frye were at the bottom of the Adriatic Sea.

It took 30 minutes with the wind at their backs in the rough seas to return to the amphibious assault ship and another five to bring the RIB onboard. Once secured, a medic escorted Moretti, Han Li, and Jehona to sickbay, where they offered the ex-Army Ranger an ice pack to hold against his swollen face. He refused it, saying he'd experienced worse from Temuujin Kundek in Mongolia. No one except for Han Li knew what that meant. She smiled.

After the three were discharged and given dry clothing, one of the crew took them to the conference room where the surviving SEAL team members were chowing down on sandwiches, potato salad, coleslaw, and chips. At the far end of the table was a row of bottled water, an air-pot of coffee, and a tray piled with brownies. Everyone was eating in near silence, losing Hunter and Frye weighing heavily on them.

Han Li sat Jehona down at the table and brought her a plate of food while Moretti got two cups of coffee. He sat down and placed one in front of Han Li. Neither was hungry after hearing that the two SEALs gave their lives to save them.

When the door opened and Captain Ruebensaal, followed by Hunter and Frye, entered the room, the mood instantly changed to one of jubilation.

"How are you both still alive, LT?" Kirk asked. "We saw the explosions."

"I'll let Captain Ruebensaal explain."

That explanation detailed the Sentinel's detection of two Hinds and the transmission of its video feed to the *Marco Island's* CIC along with the Hind's speed, heading, and other data. The captain said he attempted to contact the attack aircraft on both the international VHF & UHF guard frequencies. When that failed, and given these were fast aircraft, he said there was no time to consult higher authority on the rules of engagement. Needing to act immediately to protect the SEALs and the noncombatant crew members, although he later learned that noncombatant was not a word he should have used, he ordered the launch of the ship's RIM-116 Rolling Airframe Missiles, referred to as the RAM. With a speed above Mach two, it took out both Hinds and intercepted the missiles they'd launched.

"Once the threat was secure," Ruebensaal said, "one of the Venom helicopters that were previously launched picked up these two derelicts along with the *Green Harbor* survivors, who are now are in the brig."

The captain then described how his XO took another Venom to the human trafficking ship and conducted a maritime safety inspection to determine if it was seaworthy enough to be towed to port.

"Unfortunately, someone opened the seacocks to scuttle the vessel. The closure mechanism controls were disabled, making it impossible to prevent it from sinking," What he failed to mention was who opened the seacocks and disabled the closure mechanism. Fortunately, saltwater would destroy the XO's fingerprints.

Once Ruebensaal finished, Moretti asked to use an encrypted phone. The captain handed him his.

"Why don't you three come to my cabin when you finish with your call. There are a few things we need to sort out."

The captain sat on a thickly padded and relatively new brown leather chair in his quarters while his guests sat on the worn brown leather couch across from him.

"Tell me what's going on. What makes the three of you important enough for the Secretary of the Navy to order this ship to rescue you at all costs?"

"You received that message?" Moretti asked, his look showing he had a good idea who called the secretary. "You didn't mention the secretary when giving your rationale for shooting down the Hinds."

"It was in a captain's eyes only message that I received after the first transmission."

"Meaning you couldn't tell anyone."

"Correct. I let them assume I made the call."

The conversation stopped when Ruebensaal's phone rang. No number was displayed on his LED screen.

"Captain Ruebensaal."

It was President Ballinger. The captain listened, speaking only at the end to thank the president for the call. He looked at Moretti.

"You were behind this call?"

Moretti confirmed he was. "What did the president say?"

"What occurred was classified and on a need-to-know basis, and that only he and those in this room need to know. He also said the navy would award the *Marco Island* a Meritorious Unit Commendation. I know very few people who can speak to the president immediately. Are you military?"

"I was a former Army Ranger before a helo crash ended that career."

"And what exactly do you and your partner do?" he asked, turning his gaze on Han Li.

"We're bean counters in the White House Statistical Analysis Division."

"From a Ranger to an accountant. That stretches the envelope of credibility since I don't know any bean counter with enough influence to have the navy issue a Meritorious Unit Commendation to a ship before an after-action report is filed. I take it you did this so that my chain of command had no choice but to concur with my actions. Otherwise, they'd be contradicting both the Secretary of the Navy and the commander-in-chief - something only someone who'd been in the military would know."

"You needed the ultimate CYA."

"I'm skeptical you're bean counters but grateful for what you've done."

"In that case, maybe we could impose on your hospitality and have one of your helicopters transport Han Li and me to an island. It's where the *Green Harbor* was taking us."

"Which island?"

"Corfu. Specifically, the northeastern coast near the village of Nissaki."

"You want to go where you were being taken as a hostage? Why?"

"I need to steal something."

"If I say no, I know I'll receive a call from the president or Secretary of the Navy reversing that decision. When do you want to leave?"

"After dark. I need to do a few things first."

"I want to go," Jehona said.

"Too dangerous," Han Li responded.

"I know where you need to go on the island. You have no chance of finding it without me."

"You could tell us."

"I could, but I won't," she said stubbornly.

Han Li and Moretti admitted that there was almost a zero chance of finding what they were after without her.

"You're walking into the lion's den with a hunk of raw meat in your hand," the captain said in a concerned tone. "and taking this young lady with you. If these people have the resources to buy missile-carrying Hind attack helicopters, they're not hiring mall cops to protect their assets. I was ordered to protect the three of you, but I can't put boots on the ground in a foreign country where they might be in an armed conflict. Greece is a strategically important ally; the stakes will be high. However, if someone in the hierarchy above me orders boots on the ground, it's done."

A moment of silence followed, after which Moretti leaned forward.

"Officially, as far as you're concerned, we don't exist. Han Li and I are used to situations like this, entering alone with minimal to no support. Jehona is our responsibility."

"Good, I was afraid a support request would interfere with this ship conducting a more thorough search of the area for *Green Harbor* survivors. I calculate that will take a day or two. Since the *Marco Island* will be in the area, if the White House Statistical Analysis Division gets into trouble, as a courtesy, I'll try and help."

"That's much appreciated," Moretti said. "What we're about to do could get very messy."

"Judging from what's happened, I'm don't doubt it."

When Tosku heard the *Green Harbor* sank and he'd lost two Hind helicopters, he went into a rage. "Bring Panos Gavril to me," he screamed to his enforcer, Bardyhl Gashi. "He's responsible for the security of my ships and aircraft. Before I kill him, I want to hear why I have a ship at the bottom of the Adriatic along with my Hinds, and another ship is being auctioned."

Gashi left the study and returned 30 minutes later without Gavril. "The guards at the front gate said that he left several hours ago. His clothes and other personal items are still in his room."

"If he thinks he can leave my employ without paying for his negligence, he's wrong. Put a bounty of 200,000 euros on his head and text that with his photo to everyone who's ever received a drachma from me," Tosku said, referring to an ancient Greek currency.

Gashi got as far as the door to the study when he heard Tosku telling him to wait.

"I won't accept a photograph or statement that he's dead. I need irrefutable confirmation." Tosku told him what that entailed.

It was seven in the morning when the most senior of the town's five police officers, who was no string bean and was close to popping two buttons on his uniform shirt, walked into the local diner and took his usual seat at the counter. Kymi was a coastal town on the Greek island of Euboea with a population of 7,112. It was long known to be a bastion of privacy, inherited from its days as a major smuggling hub. The officer didn't order. The server, who was in her 60s and tipped the scales slightly under the officer's weight, had worked there for 20 years and knew what he wanted because he ate there every morning and always had the same breakfast. As soon as she saw him come through the door, she asked the cook for three eggs over medium covered with staka, which was similar to clotted cream. She prepared the rest of the order because the officer liked his eggs accompanied by two slices of especially thick crusty country bread smothered with fig jam. She also made him Greek coffee. Most of those who ate in the diner were regulars and, although the food was good, it wasn't great. They ate there because it was the only place to get a meal or buy food within a seven-mile radius.

It took the officer 45 minutes to consume his meal. He'd just downed the last of his coffee when Panos Gavril entered and took a seat at a corner table. The officer instantly recognized him, having received a text message with his photo, along with the criteria for the bounty. Not giving Gavril a second glance for fear that he'd know he'd been recognized, the officer paid his check and went to his squad car, which was parked beside the diner. He waited.

Thirty minutes later, Gavril left the repository of average food. The officer, who was leaning against his squad car, quickly approached. Pointing his gun squarely at the man's chest, he told him he was under arrest. He then handcuffed and walked Gavril to the police car, throwing him in the back before anyone saw what happened.

It took 15 minutes to get to a rocky part of the island that was bad for fishing, hiking, and smuggling because of the waves and jagged rocks. It was therefore avoided by locals and deserted except for the occasional lost tourist.

Adhering to the instructions he'd received, the officer dragged Gavril from the back of the vehicle and put a bullet in his head. It took ten minutes to provide the proof that Tosku demanded, sending a photograph of the severed head and his bank account information to Gashi. An hour later, the officer received confirmation the money was deposited in his account.

CHAPTER 8

T
HE VILLAGE OF Nissaki lies on the northeastern coast of the Greek island of Corfu and is approximately ten miles from Sarande, Albania. Taken to the island on a Venom helicopter - Moretti, Han Li, and Jehona stepped off their transport behind a hill that overlooked the wharf. Wearing night-vision goggles, the three could navigate without difficulty in the darkness that enveloped the area.

Jehona saw the village's name on a sign as she stepped off the boat which brought her here. Earlier revealing its identity, she didn't provide directions on how to get to the holding facility to which they brought her - which was her ticket to accompany Moretti and Han Li to Corfu and was an essential part of their plan.

Moretti and Han Li carried a Sig Sauer P226 9mm pistol in a shoulder holster and had an Ontario MK 3 knife and scabbard strapped to their right leg. Each carried a rucksack, which was essentially a large and rugged backpack. It contained items they'd requested, and Ruebensaal authorized the ship's supply officer to issue.

"Just to be clear," Moretti said to Jehona. "We're not here to rescue anyone. Once we get what we want, we'll inform the Greek authorities and let them send a rescue team. Our priority is to get Tosku's computer records."

"Okay," she replied, matter-of-factly.

"If the person in charge of the computer system believes the building is under siege, there's a possibility he'll smash or erase the hard drive. If that happens, we won't find out where Tosku is hiding those he's trafficking or have the evidence to shut down his operation and send him to prison," Han Li added.

Moretti stepped away to unpack his rucksack. When he did, Han Li pulled Jehona aside.

"Once you leave the dock, there are no lights in the area. Even the vehicle you were in had windows; how could you remember the route to the place they took you?"

Jehona didn't answer but looked down.

"Tell me why you wanted to come with us."

Jehona looked her in the eyes. "Because I'll never lose my fear that these men will someday kill or kidnap and sell me to the most horrid creature on earth in revenge for what I've done unless I see them destroyed," she bluntly responded.

Han Li looked at Moretti, who overheard what they said. Both knew she'd duped them into bringing her.

"I would have done the same," Han Li said.

Moretti shook his head in agreement and, with a slight smile, knew he'd made the right call when he approached Hunter before stepping onto the Venom.

Just as in Rafina, Moretti and Han Li understood the problem with staking out Tosku's operation was that he didn't provide his schedule of activities ahead of time, and it also assumed that he didn't suspend or move his operations to another island or country in response to recent setbacks. If the kidnappers were coming with their human cargo, they could wait it out for several days, bringing sleeping bags and enough food to sustain them for that time, and a combination desalination and reverse osmosis filtration pump providing purified water. However, since Corfu was 237 square miles, there was little chance of finding where they kept Jehona prisoner unless they followed the vehicle transporting the new arrivals. If they lost it, they might not have the supplies or support to wait for the next shipment of the forgotten to arrive.

Moretti's military experience taught him to take nothing for granted, which included Jehona remembering the route to her prison. Since the Sentinel had to refuel, he asked Hunter how the SEALs would track a vehicle, probably at night, without using an aerial platform as sophisticated as the Sentinel. The SEAL team commander didn't answer. Instead, he took him to the secure storage area they assigned the SEALs while on the ship. Inside a room with keypad access, the team kept their arms and equipment. Opening the door and going to a locker, he removed a rucksack containing an RQ-11B Raven drone and handed it to Moretti. The 4.2-pound UAS, or unmanned aerial system, was three feet long and had foldable wings that extended to a length of four-and-a-half feet. With a speed of up to 50 mph and a ceiling of 14,000 feet, it provided real-time color and infrared imagery to the handheld computer console containing the flight controls. Hunter then took him on deck and showed him how to operate it.

Moretti removed the drone from its rucksack and prepared it for flight.

The kidnapper's boat entered the wharf just after midnight. Han Li awoke Jehona, who was asleep, to see what was happening. The vessel wasn't big, but it was large enough to carry fourteen children - nine girls and five boys, who appeared somewhere between ten and twelve years of age. There were also three girls in their late teens. All huddled in fear.

Once the boat docked, the three men on board, all of whom carried assault rifles, forced their captives onto the dock and herded them into a windowless van. Moretti, who was watching through night vision goggles, ground his teeth. Picking up the Raven, he launched it and used the joystick to take the drone to an altitude of 500 feet, looking at its clear infrared feed on the console he was holding. The UAS followed the van to a compound in the gently sloping hills that were 1.7 miles north of the wharf. The 100-acre parcel consisted mainly of mature olive trees, which was not surprising since olive oil was Corfu's leading export and considered by master chefs to be among the best in Greece.

There were two structures within the compound - a two-story mansion and an adjoining two-story rectangular building. A decorative iron gate protected a half-mile-long gravel drive that led to the structures. The perimeter of the property had a four-foot-high dilapidated wooden fence around it. Beyond that, there was no visible security. It looked like many other olive growing businesses in the area to anyone passing the estate, something that Tosku went to great pains to ensure.

The van stopped in front of the building next to the mansion, and they took the forgotten inside. The Raven circled for another five minutes but, when it looked like nothing more would happen, Moretti touched the return home button, and the UAS banked to starboard and set course for the signal emanating from the console he was holding. The drone's landing, which relied on the operator's skill, left a lot to be desired. Thankfully, the landing gear was rugged and survived several authoritative impacts with the earth before it came to a stop 50 yards beyond the spot where Moretti intended it to land. The only evidence that its return was less than perfect was the long scrape along the fuselage where it brushed a rock. Six inches left, and the port wing would have ripped from the fuselage.

"Time to get moving," Moretti said as he returned the Raven to his rucksack. "Jehona, I know you don't want to hear this, but it's going to get extremely dangerous, and there's a likelihood that people will shoot at us. Stay here, and I promise we'll come back for you."

Her stubborn expression showed she would not play by those rules. She turned and faced Han Li, who was to Moretti's left. "You know why I need to go and why I'm not staying here without you. If you leave, I'll follow. We're wasting time," Jehona said, a response that sounded like she was the third adult in the group.

"Then let's get ready," Han Li replied, putting an end to the discussion. Taking off her rucksack, she pushed aside a couple of sleeping bags and removed two M4A1 Carbines and four mags of ammo - handing Moretti his weapon and spare rounds.

An hour and a half later, they set their gear down behind a large tree 100 yards from the gate guarding the drive. Moretti carried Jehona on his shoulders for slightly over two-thirds of their journey, even though the teenager wanted to walk. He did this so that she wouldn't be exhausted by the time they got to the compound. He also did it because he knew that depth perception was an issue when wearing night-vision goggles for a prolonged period. Therefore, he didn't want Jehona's inexperience with the goggles to get her hurt by tripping or stepping into a hole on the uneven terrain. To get her to agree to hop on his back, the ex-Army Ranger said they could move faster if she did since his and Han Li's strides were longer than hers. She agreed.

"Jehona, did you notice any cameras inside the building or on the property?" Han Li asked.

"I wasn't looking for them. Sorry."

"How about computers?"

"One."

"Do you remember where it was?"

"On the first floor, because our dormitory was on the second."

"That cuts the search area in half."

"Ready?" Moretti asked Han Li after re-launching the Raven and bringing it to altitude.

"As we agreed, if I'm captured or killed, get Jehona back to the carrier and forget about me."

Moretti wasn't wild about the idea of leaving his partner in the hands of Tosku's men but said he'd do what she asked.

Han Li hopped over the fence. Almost instantaneously, an alarm sounded, and the property became brightly lit. The LED floodlights, placed unobtrusively throughout the compound, were now visible.

"Motion detectors," Moretti said to himself as he looked at the feed from the Raven and saw Han Li running towards the front gate. As she ran, she tore her clothes and disheveled her hair. Emerging from the olive grove, two men tacked her.

Not resisting her captors, they tied her hands behind her back with a belt that one of them was wearing. Moments later, a pickup truck pulled beside them, and they threw her in the open cargo area.

"They're going to kill her," Jehona replied, the fear clear in her voice as she looked over Moretti's shoulder at the Raven's console.

"Believe me when I tell you they've let the fox into the henhouse."

As Han Li entered the building, escorted by the two men who captured her, a thin man approached. He was five feet, ten inches tall and had a well-maintained black stubble beard. Judging from the way the others backed off, it was apparent that he was the person in charge. The thin man slapped her hard across the left side of her face, the blow sending her to the ground. She was roughly pulled to her feet by one of the men who brought her into the building.

"I don't recall that you arrived with the others," the thin man said. "Where have you been hiding? Someone as attractive and exotic as you will fetch five or ten times what the scabs bring. Take her to my room," the thin man said to the person who held Han Li tightly by the arm.

There were 14 rooms on the bottom floor, seven aside. The thin man's room was the last one on the right, and the person who brought her there opened the unlocked door and shoved her inside. The thin man was a few steps behind.

The room, measuring 20 by 30 feet, had no dividers except for the bathroom. It had a couch and TV area in the front and a bedroom and bathroom in the rear. Once he entered the room and closed the door, the thin man dragged Han Li to the bed and threw her down. Grabbing her breast was the last thing he'd remember because, in the blink of an eye, she put her fist into the left side of his jaw, fracturing his mandible and dislodging two teeth. He was down for the count.

Rummaging through his quarters for a computer, she came up empty. She continued her search next door. That room was also unlocked. It was a duplicate of the thin man's quarters, except with men's clothing haphazardly cast about; it also lacked a computer. She surmised these were employee living quarters - an empty room indicating that person was working.

Three rooms later, she still hadn't found a computer or come face-to-face with anyone. That changed upon entering the next-to-last room on that side of the hall. As she walked in, she saw a guard having his way with one of the three older girls who'd arrived that evening. Seeing Han Li, he took the knife he held to the young woman's throat and threw it at her. It landed at her feet. Picking it up, she approached the rapist and handed it back. The gesture was apparent - try me. The rapist took her up on it. Taking the knife, he lunged forward and tried to bury the blade in her torso. Han Li stepped back, pushed his arm aside, whipped her right leg around, and planted her foot in the man's throat crushing his Adam's apple.

Pulling the body off the bed and onto the floor, she told the young woman to get dressed and get back to her quarters. The woman, who was crying and traumatized, and spoke a Slavic language unfamiliar to Han Li, didn't understand. Eventually, using hand gestures, she got the message.

In the last room on that side of the hall, she found another guard having his way with one of the arriving women and dispatched him by breaking his neck. The woman he was raping spoke English. Crying but appearing less traumatized than the person in the next room, Han Li gave her the same instructions.

Going across the hall, she attempted to open the door but found it locked. None of the others were. Knocking to see if someone was in the room, no one responded. She kicked the area beside the door's lock, producing the hatchet-on-kindling sound of the frame breaking apart. As the door flew open, an alarm sounded. Looking inside, she saw a laptop sitting in the middle of the desk.

Moretti and Jehona heard an alarm coming from the building into which they took Han Li.

"I think the fox is leaving the henhouse," Moretti said as he focused the Raven's camera on the building. As he said this, the lights again came on.

They saw Han Li sprinting out the front door, chased by two men shooting at her with their handguns.

"We'd better get moving," Moretti said. Telling Jehona to hold onto the console, he took the satphone from his pocket, called Ruebensaal, and requested an urgent exfil, short for exfiltrate, and said it would be hot. Looking at Raven's computer console over her shoulder, he gave rendezvous coordinates that were a mile east of their current position - far enough away from Tosku's estate so that the noise from the helicopter wouldn't give away their position, but not so far that it would take them long to get there. Once Ruebensaal confirmed that he'd divert a Venom that was on patrol, the call ended.

Moretti, getting better with his landings, recovered the Raven and returned it to his rucksack. Twenty seconds later, Han Li hopped over the fence.

"Our exfil is a mile to the east." Without further explanation, they took off with Jehona atop Moretti's shoulders.

Unknown to them, Tosku's number two in command told the guards to run to their vehicles and begin their search to the east, the direction in which Han Li ran. His orders were unambiguous - they were to kill the woman and anyone with her.

When Moretti set the exfil point, he was in a hurry and didn't notice a road less than 100 yards away. Unfortunately, as the Venom was descending, two guards in a pickup saw it and started firing at the aircraft.

The Venom helicopter was a top-of-the-line combat aircraft that had many configurations. The *Marco Island's* model had 12.7 mm machine guns installed in the open doors on either side and Hydra laser-guided anti-armor missile pods attached to the fuselage. However, Ruebensaal ordered the aircraft commander not to employ these weapons while he was over or on Greek soil, even if he received hostile fire that endangered the aircraft. The mission was to exfil three civilians, not to harm a foreign national on their native soil - even if they were the scum of the earth, which Ruebensaal said he assumed they were.

The aircraft commander, who'd seen his share of combat in Afghanistan, didn't like it - but orders were orders. He'd been in the military long enough to know, however, that he could stretch those to the breaking point so long as the rubber band didn't snap. Subsequently, as he descended into a hail of gunfire, he interpreted Ruebensaal's words, "hostile fire that endangered the aircraft," to be non-applicable in this situation since the small arms fire he received deflected off the Venom, designed to resist small-caliber rounds. Therefore, not only didn't the Venom depart the area, but it continued its descent.

"Get her on board," Moretti said to Han Li as the helicopter was 100 feet over them and continuing to descend. "I got this."

Taking his M4A1 carbine off his shoulder, he didn't wait for a response. He began peppering the truck with bullets, some of which pierced the steel doors the bad guys were hiding behind, forcing them to take cover in the heavy vegetation beside the road. Han Li grabbed Jehona, and they ran for the copter, which just set down.

Moretti continued to keep the two men pinned down with short three-round bursts, slapping in another magazine after expending the first. Once he saw they were on the aircraft, he ran for the Venom's open door while Han Li gave him covering fire. However, when it became apparent that she didn't have as good an angle on the assailants as Moretti, the two guards became emboldened and stood to get a better shot at the aircraft, bouncing their rounds off the engine housing and the cockpit. Moretti had no sooner leaped into the helicopter than a guard succeeded with a Hail Mary shot, his round finding an exposed cable tucked below the bullet-resistant equipment boxes.

"Houston, we have a problem," the aircraft commander yelled to Moretti and Han Li. "The aircraft isn't handling worth a shit. Hold on tight."

As the Venom bucked and swayed like a mechanical bull in a Texas bar, the two pilots tried to work around the problem and stabilize the aircraft. During this time, Han Li held on tightly to Jehona's vest with one hand and a side strap affixed to the bulkhead. Moretti, who was sitting across from her, had his eyes closed. Breathing heavily and sweating profusely, he had a death grip on his side strap and the front of his metal seat. He would later tell Han Li that the aircraft's violent movements dragged him back to the helicopter crash that killed everyone in his squad except for himself and Cray. That led to one year in rehab and a medical discharge from the Rangers.

As the pilots were wrestling with the aircraft, the Venom spun 180 degrees and banked hard to port. Han Li helplessly watched as Jehona slipped out of her vest and fell from the helicopter. Still holding the vest in her hand, she followed the teen as she hit the heavy brush by the side of the road - an area illuminated by the truck's headlights. Jehona, surviving the fall unharmed, looked up at Han Li. Almost immediately, the two men who'd been firing at the aircraft grabbed her.

"Go back," Han Li yelled to the flight crew. "We lost the girl."

Moretti opened his eyes.

"We're all dead if we do," the pilot responded. "This aircraft is barely controllable. We'll be lucky to make it to the ship. Put on your five-point harness; it's going to be a rough ride."

"We have to get her back," Han Li said to Moretti. "We're all she has."

"Any idea on how we do that?"

"One," she answered, removing a laptop from the small of her back.

CHAPTER 9

"**T**HE EXCHANGE WILL take place one hour and forty minutes from now," Ambassador Pullen said as he sat at a makeshift desk in his quarters. "According to the message delivered by a taxi driver, if you hand over the laptop, they'll return Jehona. However, they were clear that if they even suspect that anyone but the two of you is near the exchange site, they'll kill her."

"If these lowlifes harm or don't give Jehona back as promised, I'll find and kill everyone involved," Han Li said with a resolve that made it known that's precisely what would happen.

"I can tell you from experience," Moretti said, "you can take that statement to the bank. Not to change the subject but thank you for getting us off the ship and here so quickly. How did Tosku know you could get ahold of us?"

"I'm sure he believes you use the embassy as your home base in Athens. He manifested that belief when his men destroyed a good part of the embassy compound trying to kill you."

Moretti shook his head in acknowledgment.

"I've spoken to Captain Ruebensaal. He's developed a fondness for you two and came up with something he calls Plan B. Want to hear it?"

They said they did.

Pullen told them.

Moretti was the first to speak. "It might work. Let's hope this doesn't end with us returning to the states in an urn."

The ambassador shrugged in a manner suggesting that could happen.

"Is there a way to copy what's on the computer's hard drive before we hand it over?" Han Li asked, changing the subject.

"You told me that when you turned it on, there was a login box."

Han Li verified that's what she said.

"I don't know if copying the data is possible; there's someone who will. It should be no surprise the CIA operates from this embassy. Thankfully, their lab wasn't in one of the buildings destroyed in the missile attack. Let me ask if their tech will help because I have no control over what the agency does." He made the call, giving Han Li a thumbs up during the conversation.

It was the first time she smiled since losing Jehona.

Pullen gave her directions to the lab, saying she needed to be back within thirty minutes so she and Moretti could take the helicopter to the exchange site.

The message that Pullen received didn't expressly state that the exchange was to take place at the Cave of the Lakes. Instead, it provided GPS coordinates that corresponded with the nondescript jagged vertical rip in the mountain's side that proved to be its entrance. Located six miles from the village of

Kleitoria and approximately 136 miles from Athens, its name came from the fact that the melting winter snow created a subterranean river within the cave, replete with waterfalls. However, in the summer, this river dried up and left behind 13 lakes. The cave was nearly a mile-long and had within it a labyrinth of 60 corridors and many galleries.

The Bell 407 Textron helicopter the ambassador provided set down near the rip in the mountain at the appointed time. The area appeared deserted as Moretti and Han Li left the aircraft. Approaching the entrance, they saw a large red piece of paper under a rock. On it was instructions, written in English, that directed them to follow the lights.

Walking through the jagged portal, which had a height of approximately 30 feet and a width of 12, they saw LED lights evenly spaced atop the stone pathway, enabling them to see where they were going in the otherwise absolute darkness of the cave. Following them, they veered through several side tunnels before entering a well-lit circular chamber that was 30 yards in diameter. Jehona was standing beside Bardyhl Gashi and Taulant Manjani.

"Is the Albanian government complicit in this?" Moretti asked, unable to resist throwing a dart at Manjani.

"Mr. Manjani works for my employer. If the three of you hadn't escaped on your way to Corfu, you would have experienced his unparalleled expertise as an interrogator. If that occurred, I doubt your attitude towards him would be this cavalier Getting to business, did you bring the computer?"

Han Li removed it from the small of her back, then held it in the air for Gashi to see.

"Turn it on?" Gashi ordered.

She did, and the logon screen appeared.

"Place it on the ground and walk away."

"Not until we have the girl," Moretti said in a voice that indicated giving them the computer was contingent upon handing over Jehona.

"You gave up whatever leverage you had when you docilely got off your aircraft and walked in here. Why don't I kill all three of you and take the computer?" Tosku's assassin asked as he removed a Czech nine-millimeter pistol from the shoulder holster under his jacket. "That sounds like a much better plan. Afterward, I'll throw your bodies into a lake. They won't discover you until the spring runoff."

"I have a better idea," Moretti retorted. "We both leave with what we came for, and you get to live."

Gashi was confused by what he'd heard, while Manjani's face was impassive. "I'm the one with the gun," Tosku's assassin replied.

"Look outside the cave."

The calm and confident expression on Moretti's face was unsettling to Gashi. He told Manjani to have a look, after which he grabbed the girl by the arm and pointed his gun at her head.

The interrogator ascended a lightweight steel ladder in the chamber's corner that led to a ledge ten feet above them, then disappeared through a barely visible opening. He returned five minutes later. The worried expression on his face said it all.

"What?" Gashi asked in a gruff voice.

"There's two heavily armed US military helicopters circling the area. One of them saw me and started in my direction as I came back inside."

"I was clear that I'd kill the girl if I even suspected you brought someone with you," Gashi said to Moretti, giving him a look that showed he was contemplating doing just that.

"Then you might as well point the gun at your head and pull the trigger because one of those helicopters belongs to SEAL Team 4. Unless the three of us walk out of here, they'll come looking for us. You have," Moretti said, looking at his watch, "exactly 15 minutes until they enter the cave. Neither of you will survive the encounter since they were told you're terrorists and not to take prisoners."

From the look on both Gashi's and Manjani's faces, Moretti's bluff was working. Contrary to what he'd said, Pullen told him that Ruebensaal's Plan B was that the Venom's would be there only as a show of force and that he could concoct any story he wanted regarding their presence.

"How do I know we'll be free to leave if I hand over the girl?"

"Unlike you, I keep my word. The clock is ticking. Your handguns won't fare well against a SEAL team and two combat helicopters."

The expression on Gashi's face showed he would have loved to kill Moretti, Han Li, and Jehona, but that his survival came first. Shoving the girl in the back, he pushed her towards them. Han Li grabbed her.

"We'll go up the ladder and exit first. Once we're gone, it'll be safe for you both to leave," Moretti said.

Han Li laid the laptop on the ground and was the first to ascend, followed by Jehona and Moretti.

As they exited what they believed to be a smuggler's portal, they followed a dirt path that led to the cave's entrance. The helicopter pilot, waiting in the same spot where he touched down, saw them and brought the aircraft to life. A short time later, they were back at the US embassy in Athens.

Tosku listened patiently to Gashi's explanation of how the three people he'd ordered executed had escaped; his anger kept in check only because he held the stolen computer. Manjani, who was standing to the right of the assassin, confirmed his story.

"They'll try to leave the country as soon as possible and take the girl with them. Since she needs an Albanian passport, that gives us time to put together a plan to kill them before they get on a flight."

"I know how we can do that, but it'll be messy," Gashi said.

"Blowing up the American embassy without killing your targets was messy. Handing over the girl and not killing everyone was messy. Make sure you succeed this time. You won't get a third chance."

Gashi's expression showed that he understood the implications of failure.

As both men watched, Tosku turned on the computer and typed in the twelve-digit alpha/numeric/symbol password. He then checked the access log, a customized feature installed by his programmer to allow him to see the last time someone accessed or copied a file or folder. Everyone within his organization had separate logins, which only granted access to data relevant to their jobs. He was the only one with unrestricted entry.

As Tosku studied the log, he slammed his fist down on his desk so hard that it jarred the computer. A string of expletives followed. "They accessed this computer."

"How?" Gashi asked.

"It doesn't matter; what does is that have a copy of this hard drive," Tosku retorted in a voice filled with rage.

Opening his desk drawer, he pulled out a Glock 19 handgun. "Let me give you my definition of messy," Tosku said, looking Gashi squarely in the eye as he put a bullet into his head.

Manjani jumped aside to avoid the body, which fell backward onto the floor.

"Surround the embassy with enough eyes to keep track of the whereabouts of the three who escaped. If they leave, follow them and report back. Is that clear?"

Glancing at Gashi's body, Manjani returned his gaze to Tosku and said those instructions were clear.

"What did Crenshaw have to say?" Moretti asked, referring to the US Secretary of State, as Pullen entered the makeshift conference room where he and Han Li were sitting while Jehona was getting a bite to eat in the tent that served as the embassy's cafeteria. Pullen had left them to take the call.

"That he's still trying to find out who's responsible for the attack on the embassy and will lean on the Greek government to provide better intelligence and protection."

"Putting a bullet into Tosku's brain will eliminate at least one threat to the embassy."

"It may come to that. In a separate conversation, President Ballinger told me to keep your names out of any report. If your names come up, I'm to say you're in Athens on vacation and were at the embassy during the attack for reasons I'll create."

"When can we leave for the airport?" Moretti asked.

"You and Ms. Li can leave anytime. Jehona's another matter. It will take a day or two to get her an Albanian passport so she can depart the country and return home."

"Why so long?" Moretti asked.

"She's never had one, and Albanian bureaucracy, I'm told, makes ours look efficient."

"What if she doesn't want to return to the orphanage?

"She hasn't got a choice. She's an Albanian citizen. That's her home."

"Give us a second to talk about this, would you, ambassador?" Han Li asked.

"Come to my quarters when you're ready." Without waiting for a response, Pullen left and closed the door behind him.

"You know we can't leave her. Tosku will find Jehona and kill her," Han Li said.

"Unless we kill him first."

"Agreed. But that still doesn't mean that once she's back at the orphanage, some other deviate won't try to kidnap her. I have an idea how we can keep her safe. It's radical, but it'll work."

"Radical is our middle name. What's your plan?"

"Adopt her."

Moretti was surprised and took a few seconds to craft a response.

"You realize Nemesis is a quasi-military organization that requires extensive travel to places where we expect people will try and kill us. We leave at a moment's notice, and there's always the possibility that one or both of us won't come back. Also, consider that you're a Chinese citizen who lives in an ever-rotating string of hotels and motels in the Washington area while I live in the visiting officer's quarters at Site R. We don't have a home."

"To your first point, our missions usually last less than two weeks. Most less than one."

"We're still gone."

"Continuing with radical, we buy a house and send Jehona to boarding school. She'll have friends and receive a great education. Our travel won't be an issue."

"You've given this some thought."

Han Li confessed she had.

"You used the words we and our."

"Jehona needs parents, not a parent. We jointly raise her. Two single people raising a daughter isn't unusual."

Moretti walked up to Han Li, put his arms around her, and gave her a kiss that lasted much longer than he at first intended. "You know how I feel about you and how I have a hard time expressing that feeling."

"Fear of rejection?"

"It's a male thing. The fact is, I'm addicted to you and Jehona. Two unmarried people raising a daughter - I'm in."

"Let's talk to her and see how she feels. She has the last word."

They went to Pullen's quarters and requested that he have someone bring Jehona there. The ambassador tasked the marine standing outside his room with making that happen after she'd finished eating. "What do you want to do?" Pullen asked once he'd given those instructions.

"Han Li and I, subject to Jehona's approval, want to adopt her and take her back to the US with us."

Pullen wasn't surprised.

"I can't think of two people I'd trust more to raise her. I'm already feeling sorry for the first boy she tries to date. Does this mean you're tying the knot?"

"No. We're raising her as single parents," Han Li said. "We're not getting married."

"Right," Pullen said with a tone of finality that indicated it was the last time he intended to ask that question.

Fifteen minutes later, there was a knock on the door, after which the marine opened it and allowed Jehona to enter. Han Li approached the fourteen-year-old.

"Jehona, Matt and I have a question. Take your time before you answer; make sure that you choose what's best for you. Promise?"

"Promise," she replied, looking apprehensive.

"We'd like to adopt and raise you in the United States."

Jehona didn't respond. Instead, she leaped into Han Li's arms and hugged her tightly around her neck.

"I'll take that as a yes. Leave the formalities to myself and the president. Which brings up the point: now might be a good time to tell him about the adoption," Pullen said, handing Moretti his phone.

The call with Ballinger went well, and he supported their decision. Cray, who the president conferenced onto the call, wasn't wild about the idea of his two best operatives having a daughter but supported their decision.

The president said he'd send a military aircraft to Athens and transport them to Joint Base Andrews.

"It'll take me a couple of days to get her an Albanian passport," Pullen said.

"I'll arrange the flight for the day after tomorrow," the call ending with that statement.

"The three of you might want to stay somewhere else," Pullen said. "If they lobbed two missiles into the compound once, they could do it again. I'm sure after what just happened; they'll try even harder to kill the three of you. This time, you might not be as lucky."

"Where do you suggest we hide?" Moretti asked.

"I have a friend who owns a hotel. You'll like it, and I don't think Tosku will expect you to hide there."

"How do we get out of the compound without being seen?" Han Li asked. "He'll have people watching the embassy."

"Leave that to me."

"Where are we going?" Han Li asked.

Pullen told her.

CHAPTER 10

THE HELICOPTER LIFTED off from the US embassy compound with its three passengers and turned southeast, heading towards the Aegean Sea. Jehona, who less than an hour ago learned she had a new family, found the spark of joy missing from her life and was constantly smiling. Before they left the ambassador's office, Moretti asked if she'd like to keep her last name or take his - something that he and Han Li discussed while waiting for her to arrive from the cafeteria. When she responded that Dibra had no meaning because she had no family by that name and that she'd love to take his, Moretti gave her a Cheshire grin.

"Jehona Moretti, welcome to the family."

"Where will we live?"

"Good question," Han Li answered. "We haven't thought that part through, but I would expect we'd look for a house near the capital. However, we'd like you to go to boarding school so you can get an excellent education and not be adversely affected by our sudden travel requirements."

Jehona's smile evaporated.

"Try it for a semester. If you don't like it, we'll figure something else out. You'll have the last say where you want to go to school."

Jehona's smile returned.

For the next hour, Moretti and Han Li gave their future daughter their backgrounds and family histories. Han Li omitted she was once China's premier assassin, saying only that she worked for the Chinese government. Both steered clear of mentioning Nemesis. Instead, they told her they worked for the White House Statistical Analysis Division and left it at that.

The Bell 407 Textron helicopter touched down at the Thira Airport in Santorini, Greece, an hour and thirty minutes after leaving the embassy compound. Ambassador Pullen, whose longtime friend owned the Mystique hotel in Oia, a small village carved out of the cliffs of a caldera, arranged for a car to bring them there. That journey took 30 minutes, ending when the vehicle pulled to the side of a narrow two-lane highway that passed above the hotel. As they stepped out, they saw a postcard-perfect view of stark white buildings with iconic, blue-domed roofs framed against the deep blue of the Aegean Sea. The hotel manager and a porter were waiting to greet them. The porter took their carry-on's while the manager guided them to the registration desk, the walk down the steep concrete path requiring the surefootedness of a mountain goat. When they got there, Moretti said he felt like he'd been on a Stairmaster. The female contingent of the trio was unfazed and didn't comment.

"This is your key to a two-bedroom suite," the manager said, handing it to Moretti. You have it for two nights. If you need to remain longer, let me know."

Moretti removed a credit card from his wallet and handed it and his passport to the manager.

"Neither is necessary. I'll have the porter put your bags in your room. Enjoy your stay."

"Why don't you and Jehona wait outside. I need a word with the manager," Moretti told Han Li. Once they left, he asked a favor.

"I may have found them," Manjani said, walking into a room off Tosku's bedroom where his employer was getting his hair cut.

Tosku told the stylist to wait in the hall and close the bedroom door behind him.

"Where?"

"Thira airport, Santorini. Three hours ago, one of our men called and said they saw a helicopter land at the embassy and depart minutes later. He got the tail number and gave it to me. I used our contact at the police department to trace where the aircraft went and where it'd been. He told me the US embassy previously rented this helicopter to go to the Caves of the Lakes."

"We know where they are, but why Santorini?" Tosku asked. "It's an island with limited escape options."

"Perhaps they're going to get on one of the cruise ships docking at the port of Skala."

Tosku thought for a moment before responding. "Getting onto a ship requires a passport. If the girl had one, she'd be on a plane out of Greece and not on a lumbering cruise ship. However, she doesn't need a passport or ID if she stays in the country and travels by private transport. The only explanation that makes sense is that the ambassador is trying to hide them until he can get her the necessary documents to leave the country. Do we know where they're staying?"

Manjani said he didn't.

"Have our contact look at the police database since they require hotels to send them a guest's name and their passport or national ID number. That said, I'm not optimistic their names will appear. They're smart. They'll be off the grid."

"How will we find them?"

"Text a photo of the three, just as we did with that incompetent Panos Gavril, to everyone we know on the island. Offer three levels of rewards, rather than all or none." Tosku explained the structure of the compensation.

"We don't have a photo of the American or the Asian."

"They passed through airport immigration and customs when they entered Greece. Get it from our contact. Take the photo of the girl from our database."

"And once we find them?"

"Kill them, search the bodies, and bring any computer storage device to me. Have the overpaid captain of *Hercules* go to Santorini and anchor near the midpoint of the island. He'll be my backup."

"Respectfully, if we use the *Hercules*, the damage it will cause puts the incident as the top story for every global news network. It may anger or embarrass the government enough to come after you."

"If what's on that computer gets out, I'll go to jail for the rest of my life, or one of my clients will kill me so that I can't make a deal with the government."

"They may have hidden the information they copied. If we kill them prematurely, we won't find it."

"What they have will be on a hard or flash drive and is too important not to carry with them. They're on the run. They won't have time to circle back and retrieve something. Kill them, and we'll either find the drive on one of their bodies, or it'll be destroyed with whatever happens to them. Time is of the essence. I'm not the tourist minister. Get the *Hercules* to Santorini!"

Manjani left without further comment.

"We need to do some shopping," Han Li said, looking at what Jehona was wearing and at the sorry state of their clothes.

"According to our driver, the main street in Oia is a three-minute walk from here," Moretti said. "We'll shop and get a bite to eat."

As they left their room and began the steep climb to the narrow highway, a delivery driver offloading food supplies looked closely at them before removing the phone from his pants pocket and studying the photos in the text. It was them.

Tosku offered three levels of rewards. The first was to spot the three and give their location, either a hotel room number or house address, to the person who answered the number provided. He offered a larger reward for killing them and sending proof of their demise. The most significant compensation, equivalent to ten years of wages for the average worker, was for obtaining the computer storage device that one of them carried.

The driver knew he had no chance of killing the man accompanying the two females - at least not by himself and without a weapon. But he had cousins - lots of cousins. And they had weapons. However, since they lived and worked at the opposite end of the island, and traffic was always fierce on Santorini, it would take them time to get here. Not wanting to go home empty-handed if someone else spotted them, he would guarantee himself the first level reward by finding which room they were in.

After stacking the boxes of supplies on his hand truck and delivering them to the kitchen, he stopped by the front office on his return to the truck. With the hotel manager checking rooms before new guests' arrival, her junior assistant was alone. The driver began by saying he saw a man, describing Moretti to a tee, drop a twenty euro note as he walked up the stairs. He innocently asked for his room number so that he could slide the money under his door. The assistant responded that giving out a guest's room number was against hotel policy and offered to handle it. The driver knew this and agreed, having been in the registration office before. Taking the money from him and knowing Moretti's room number since she was there when the manager handed him the key, she placed the twenty euro note in an envelope, along with a message, and put it in box number 39.

The driver returned to his truck and sent a text to Manjani giving the hotel name and room number, locking in the first reward. Once his cousins arrived, he'd lock in the second.

Thalami restaurant was halfway down the main street that bisected the village of Oia. A small family-owned business, its open terrace overlooked the caldera and afforded a beautiful view of the Aegean Sea and the southwest portion of the island. Based on the server's recommendation, they ordered the chicken souvlaki. It came with toasted pita bread and French fries. Jehona had gotten her appetite back and quickly powered through her fries, which were replenished with those from Moretti's and Han Li's plates.

As they were having lunch, the driver watched from across the way, occasionally giving updates to his cousins as they drove to Oia.

His presence didn't go unnoticed.

"Someone in the vestibule across from the restaurant is very interested in us," Moretti whispered to Han Li.

"You mean the produce driver who was delivering to our hotel when we left?"

Moretti nodded. "Why don't you pay him a visit while I stay with Jehona. Maybe he can explain his interest in us, although I think I know."

"Tosku."

Moretti again nodded. "We need to take him out of the equation after we find how long we have until the others arrive. He's watching us for a reason."

"Agreed." Han Li got up from the table and asked a server where the restroom was located. He pointed to the back, and she headed in that direction as Moretti paid the bill.

The driver, seeing through the restaurant's window a server pointing Han Li to the rear, believed she was going to the restroom and not leaving since the other two remained at the table. Focusing on them, he never saw the palm heel strike that Han Li delivered with the bottom of her hand to the bridge of his nose, instantly breaking it. The force of the blow drove him further into the vestibule - out of sight from any passerby.

When Moretti could no longer see the driver, he escorted Jehona to the taxi stand, fifty feet from the restaurant.

"I think Tosku's men know where we are. I need you to wait here while I get Han Li. Can you do that?"

Once Jehona said she could, he ran towards the vestibule, calling Pullen as he did and saying they'd been discovered and needed to get off the island as soon as possible. The ambassador didn't ask questions. Instead, he said to get everyone to the airport, and he'd handle their escape.

When Moretti found Han Li, she was standing over the unconscious driver. Blood ran from his broken nose onto his dark blue work shirt. He also saw large bruises on the sides of his face.

"Did you find out anything?"

"The driver texted one of Tosku's men and gave the name of our hotel and room number. He also said his cousins were on their way to the restaurant to kill us."

"I phoned the ambassador. He said to get to the airport, and he'd get us off the island."

"Jehona?"

"Waiting at the taxi stand across the way."

Moretti and Han Li left the unconscious driver. As they stepped into the street, they came face to face with five rough-looking men, each weighing 230 pounds plus, who seemed to recognize them. The Nemesis operatives retraced their steps into the vestibule.

The fight began when the man standing at the head of the pack took a swing at Moretti, missed, and was rebalancing when the ex-Army Ranger put his fist between his eyes and knocked him unconscious.

Han Li attacked the two men to her right. They lasted 1.2 seconds - the time to deliver a front roundhouse kick to the temple of one, followed by a side kick to the jaw of the other.

Two cousins remained. Moretti didn't choose which he was going to fight. That decision was made when one drew a switchblade and attempted to slash his face. Dancing around like a prizefighter, the cousin wielded the knife in a way that might intimidate some, but not an ex-Army Ranger with hand-to-hand combat experience. Moretti grabbed the man's knife arm and broke it by jerking it in an unnatural direction. He followed by putting a fist in his face. The last man standing saw what happened and was not about to get near this pair. Instead, not having a gun, he decided he would throw his knife at Moretti. Judging from how he held the blade, Moretti saw that this person knew what he was doing and had a decent chance of planting the blade in him.

As the last man standing slowly raised his arm and focused on Moretti's torso, he never saw Han Li approach and thrust her right foot into the side of his head.

They left the vestibule and started towards the taxi stand, seeing three men 200 yards away, who were walking towards them and clones of the five they'd just fought. Apparently, the driver came from a large family.

"We need to get out of here," Moretti said as he and Han Li shoved Jehona into a taxi.

It took less than a minute to get to the Mystique. Moretti told the driver to wait while they got their bags, handing him a twenty euro note and promising another when he returned plus the meter to the airport. The driver turned off his engine.

"Jehona, wait for us at the top of the staircase," Moretti said. "We'll be right back."

Moretti and Han Li raced down the steep steps to their room. Slightly less than half a minute later, there was a tremendous explosion.

CHAPTER 11

"**I THINK WE** can assume that Matt Moretti and Han Li, and the information they took from me, are at the bottom of the Adriatic," Tosku said, looking for the third time at the video taken by the *Hercules* of the destruction of part of the Mystique hotel. "Don't look so surprised, Taulant."

Manjani remained silent. Getting into a war of words with Tosku that criticized one of his decisions was not good for one's longevity.

"As I thought about it, the longer they stayed alive, the more risk I had. With the United States government helping them, I may not have gotten another chance to kill them and destroy what they stole from me. That's why I had the *Hercules* put a missile through their hotel window."

Jehona, who was captured by the three men arriving too late to help their cousins, listened in silence, her arms and legs bound to a chair in the basement of Tosku's residence.

"Your two saviors are dead. Tomorrow, I'll make an example of you to show what happens to anyone who even thinks about escaping. Before then, you're going to tell me how you escaped my safe house and give me the name of anyone who helped."

Jehona remained silent; the look on her face was no longer scared but defiant.

"I love a challenge," Tosku said, removing a needle, syringe, and vial from his desk drawer. "This serum is called SP-117 and was developed by the Russians. I've found it far more reliable than psychoactive drugs like scopolamine. Time to find out what you know."

The Prime Minister of Greece, Georg Petrakis, was an honest politician who cared deeply for the people of his country - a philosophy that was anathema to the political elite who spent more time trying to find a vacation home in the mountains than putting the same effort into creating jobs that would allow people to feed and clothe their families. He spent most of his time trying to shore up his country's flagging economy.

That priority was subordinated to the number two position with the missile attacks on the US embassy and the Mystique hotel. Since tourism accounted for approximately 20 percent of the country's GDP, and people don't come to countries where missiles slammed into hotels, he was determined to take whatever actions were necessary to prevent another attack from occurring. Roasted in the media more than usual, there was talk in parliament of throwing him out on his ass if another attack occurred or he failed to capture those responsible.

Despite the press reporting that terrorists were behind the attacks, which he didn't trust because there was no proof corroborating this, he believed the perpetrator was Behar Tosku. He based this assumption on the late Colonel Defrim Kote's report, which credited two foreigners, Matt Moretti and Han Li, with providing the information necessary to close two of Tosku's trafficking safe houses and the confiscation of one of his ships. Therefore, he didn't believe it was a coincidence that they were within the embassy compound and at the Mystique during those missile attacks. Instead, he suspected Tosku was trying to kill them for costing him a great deal of money and damaging his reputation. He was also sure that Kote's relationship with the foreigners led to his death.

Because shell companies and offshore corporations shielded Tosku's culpability, and he didn't use electronic devices that could be monitored or hacked, it was unlikely there would ever be enough evidence to charge him in a court of law. For that, there needed to be incontrovertible proof of his illegalities and someone credible who could stay alive long enough to testify against him. Petrakis dreamed about this irrefutable evidence. As it turned out, it came from an unexpected source.

Jehona's interrogation was over in 20 minutes, Tosku discovering that no one helped her escape, and a lapse in security was to blame. He also learned that her now-deceased saviors were going to adopt her and that she would live in the United States. That wasn't going to happen because, before long, she'd be joining them.

"When do you want to kill her?" Manjani asked.

"Once the drugs wear off, and she's fully awake. I need her alert and frightened when I begin the torture. The pain in her face and her screams will carry it from there. At her age, she'll last at least 30 minutes. Is the camcorder ready?"

Manjani confirmed it was, pointing to the Canon XA50 atop the tripod behind him.

"After her death, we'll deal with the prime minister. He's become more troublesome than usual. These missile attacks have fired him up. I can't let his fury against me become infectious. I want a prime minister who's supportive of my business interests."

"What would you like me to do?"

"The terrorists who attacked the embassy and the hotel are going to put an RPG into the side of the prime minister's vehicle. Once he's dead, I'll make a deal with one of the frontrunners for that office and put enough money behind them, so they win. Get the prime minister's schedule, figure out the best location for the attack, and put together something on the terrorist organization we're going to blame. I want to give it to his successor."

Ambassador Pullen called the Greek Minister of Foreign Affairs, Landor Andino, and requested a confidential meeting with the prime minister as quickly as possible. That request was approved. Thirty minutes later, he arrived at the Maximos Mansion, which was in central Athens near Syntagma Square. Petrakis and Andino were waiting at a circular conference table in the prime minister's office when Pullen entered. Both men rose to greet him. After a brief exchange of pleasantries, the three sat.

"Perhaps you can share the reason for this urgent meeting," Petrakis said as he leaned back in his chair.

"President Ballinger thought you might find these useful," Pullen replied, removing six, eight-by-ten-inch photographs from a folder within his polished and unscarred brown Chiarugi diplomatic briefcase. He handed them to Petrakis.

The first photo was of the *Hercules* launching the missile at the Mystique hotel; the image so clear that the serial number on the side of the missile was clearly visible. A second photo caught the missile impacting the hotel. The last four showed Jehona Dibra being held by three men as she stood near a taxi; stepping into a helicopter at the Thira airport; getting off that aircraft in Tosku's compound; and entering his residence.

"Taken from one of your spy satellites?" Andino asked.

"A drone."

Petrakis and Andino didn't ask what an unauthorized American aircraft was doing over sovereign Greek airspace, figuring it would be counterproductive to what Pullen was sharing. They'd address the issue at a later date.

"Photo number one," Pullen explained, "shows a BGM-71 TOW missile leaving its launcher. The missile's serial number matches one stolen from an ally country two years ago. In the last four photographs, the girl is Jehona Dibra, an Albanian orphan kidnapped from Tirana. She escaped from one of Tosku's safe houses and was recaptured."

"She won't be alive long," Andino said. "He'll make an example of her to terrify the others he's kidnapped. I've heard that he records the torture and gruesome deaths of those who escaped and were caught and forces every captive to watch."

"How do you know?" Pullen asked.

"We have paid informants within his organization. They're small fish."

"We need to rescue Jehona Dibra quickly before she appears in a recording."

Andino did not respond to that statement, and silence permeated the room. Petrakis broke the stalemate.

"Do you know who owns the *Hercules*?" the prime minister asked.

"A shell company with more layers than an onion."

"Do you know its current location?"

"Crete," Pullen answered, taking a photo from his briefcase and handing it to Petrakis. The image was of a small cove and showed the *Hercules* entering a fissure at the cliff's bottom. A walkway with a side rail was at the base of the opening.

"What you've shown us," Petrakis commented, "is at the very least proof of Tosku's involvement in kidnapping Jehona Dibra."

"I'm only returning photos taken by a Greek OURANOS drone."

Judging from the expressions that Petrakis and Andino had, the light went on.

"It's lucky our drone was on a training exercise over the Aegean Sea when the attack on Santorini occurred," Petrakis said. "And that it could follow the helicopter that took Jehona Dibra to Tosku's compound in Rafina. Is there anything else, Ambassador?"

"The United States would like a copy of what the police discovered at the second safe house."

"They did not inform me of any discovery," Andino said.

Petrakis, the sharper pencil in the pack, read between the lines.

"I'll ensure you get it. Could you refresh my memory as to what that was?" the prime minister asked.

"Everything on Behar Tosku's server, of course," Pullen answered to the astonished looks of both men as he opened his briefcase.

CHAPTER 12

BATTALION LEADER JORAN Karas was a member of the 32nd Marine Brigade of the Dynameis Pegonauton - Greece's Marine Corps. He was six feet, two inches tall, had a square-jaw and chiseled face, close-cropped black hair, a deep and resonant voice, and dark brown eyes that conveyed the person behind them was too serious to either understand or appreciate a joke. He had a prominent nose that was not unlike those that adorned the busts of famous Greeks such as Aristotle, Diogenes, and Strabo. At this moment, he and 59 fellow marines, four fifteen-man teams, were parachuting into Tosku's compound - a ten-acre fortress atop a 300-foot-high plateau. With nearly vertical walls surrounding it, the only ground entrance was a road leading to an I-beam reinforced gate that could withstand anything less than a 70-ton M1a2 Abrams tank. Within this road were two dozen electronically controlled stanchions, and on either side of those were a series of remotely controlled IEDs. The fortress's border atop the plateau was a ten-foot-high, six-foot thick wall constructed of steel-upgraded reinforced concrete capable of absorbing substantial tensile, shear, and compressive stresses.

There were four white stucco buildings within the compound, the largest of which was Tosku's residence - a three-story, 30,000-square-foot structure with a basement. Within the basement was a control room receiving feeds from the 200 plus security cameras that viewed virtually every square inch of his property, including the cliff and access road. The twin three-story buildings next to the residence were living quarters for security and staff. The fourth building was an armory. However, most of Tosku's weapons were in Crete within a structurally reinforced cave.

Before getting on the C-130 aircraft, Karas told his commanding officer he would have preferred the assault to happen in the early morning hours when people were asleep, and those awake were tired and less responsive, rather than a few minutes after dark. However, given that the mission was to rescue a fourteen-year-old girl in imminent danger, they abandoned the ideal assault time.

Once he rescued the hostage, and if the situation permitted, he was to apprehend Behar Tosku and those within the compound - the rub being there was no intel on his security force's size or their armament. Handed the original construction plans before stepping on the plane, he assumed they made substantial changes over the years - if the plans he held were even accurate to begin with.

Karas was the first to set foot in the compound, a klaxon sounding the instant he descended below the perimeter walls. Shortly after that, men started pouring out of the two buildings beside the principal residence, and they came under hostile fire. Karas was grazed by a round piercing his fatigues, gouging the skin on his left arm. The two men beside him weren't as fortunate. One took a bullet to the face and the other to his neck - both died. He and the twelve surviving team members sprinted to the door of Tosku's residence, where one unshouldered a sawed-off shotgun and blew away the hinges. As they entered, they could hear the fierce firefight that was going on behind them. Karas split his team. He and two men would search the basement while everyone else combed the floors above.

When the klaxon sounded, Manjani received a call from security. He turned to Tosku. "We need to leave. The military has parachuted into our compound." Even in the basement, he and Tosku could hear the firefight outside the residence.

"What we need is to kill the prime minister so we can operate without interference."

"We haven't much time."

"I hate to film her death without the torture; it won't have the same impact. But I have no other option," Tosku said, looking at Jehona, whose legs and arms they strapped tightly to the wooden chair.

"Cut her throat," Manjani said.

"A quick death doesn't generate the same fear as a lingering demise. I have a better idea."

Manjani started the camcorder as Tosku picked up a scalpel from a tray of instruments on the table.

"This will happen to anyone who even contemplates an escape," he said to the camera as he cut Jehona's right wrist. "Lamtumirë," he added, which in Albanian meant goodbye.

Manjani shut off the camera, removed it from the tripod, and ran to the room's opposite side as Tosku threw the scalpel on the table and followed. He pressed a button hidden under a steel shelf support, a row of shelves moving forward and exposing a lighted tunnel. After they entered, Manjani pressed a button that resealed the entrance.

Jehona let out a loud and piercing scream for help. But as her energy decreased with the loss of blood, her voice transformed into little more than a whisper. The life that drained from her body, starting out as a few drips on the floor, became a pool of red. Her heart was in overdrive, trying to get blood to her organs. Losing that battle, her body began to shut down, and she struggled to stay awake to keep from entering a sleep from which she would never awaken.

There were two ways out of the basement. One was to take the interior stairs. The other was through the hidden tunnel door that Tosku and Manjani took, leading to the access road. The ten security personnel in the basement control room intended to use the tunnel exit and withdrew their guns from their shoulder holders as they entered the hall, leading to the room with that exit. One inherent problem with getting there was that they needed to cross the staircase that led from the ground floor to the basement. Luck not being on their side, encountering Karas and his men. Had they thrown down their weapons and raised their hands, they would have been taken to jail and given a hard cot and awful food. However, an intellectual in the group shot at the assault team, didn't hit his target, and a shootout ensued. That didn't go well for the security team because the marines carried Heckler & Koch G3 battle rifles, while the security guards used the same type of Czech nine-millimeter pistol that Gashi carried. The guards got off three single shots, again missing their targets, while the marines had their weapons set to automatic fire mode and pressed the trigger. A cascade of bullets ended the confrontation.

Karas's team began throwing open doors, looking for Jehona and any stragglers who remained behind. They found her in the fourth room they checked. Seeing a pool of blood and that the girl was breathing but unconscious, Karas told the marine standing beside him to run and get a medic. Kneeling beside Jehona, he put pressure on the wound and raised the girl's arm above her heart to slow blood release. While he did this, the other marine removed his backpack and took out the first aid kit. Finding the Quikclot Combat Gauze, a hemostatic clotting agent, he ripped open the packet with his teeth and wrapped it tightly over the wound. Three minutes later, a medic, who was part of another fifteen-man team, arrived. He briefly removed the Quikclot and examined the wound before reapplying the gauze, gripping it firmly with his left hand.

"Her radial artery is cut, and she's obviously lost a lot of blood. She needs a transfusion, or she'll die."

"Let's find a vehicle and drive her to the hospital in Rafina," Karas said. "It'll be faster than waiting for a transport."

"That'll take too long. She's close to death and needs a transfusion now. Find someone with O Negative blood," the medic said, referring to the blood type which allowed someone to be a universal donor.

"You're looking at him."

"Roll up your sleeve."

As Karas was supplying the still unconscious Jehona with blood, the medic stitched her wrist and placed a protective bandage over it. Karas's second in command entered the room.

"The compound is secure, and our transports will set down in five minutes."

"Casualties?"

"Four dead and sixteen wounded, not counting you," he said, looking at the streak of blood on Karas's left arm where a bullet grazed him. "Five men are in serious condition."

"Get them on the first transport that lands and make sure a medic goes with them. What about casualties on the other side?"

"Twelve dead and twenty wounded. Counting the wounded, we have thirty-three prisoners."

"Get their wounded out behind ours. Tosku?"

Karas's second in command shook his head in the negative.

"Skatá."

CHAPTER 13

WITH PRESIDENT BALLINGER'S help, Jehona received her adoption and naturalization approvals in record time. Jehona Dibra became Jehona Elira Moretti, a citizen of the United States. Now that they had a daughter, Moretti and Han Li decided to buy a house to provide her with a stable living environment. With Bonaquist and Cray's help, they found their ideal residence in Hyattsville, Maryland - a 2,428-square-foot newly built home with five bedrooms and four baths. The house stretched across a 7,500-square-foot lot, which adjoined similar-sized properties. Although Hyattsville was only eleven miles from DC, sixteen miles from Bonaquist's home in Bowie, and nine miles from Cray's residence in Greenbelt, it was 75 miles from Site R. However, with the restricted access underground passageways from the Pentagon and NSA, that commute was faster than traveling to the White House.

Although the house they wanted wasn't a mansion, it was priced like one. The neighborhood was a private enclave in the woods, a desirable commodity in the DC area. Subsequently, it listed for three-quarters of a million dollars, between two to three times what Cray and Bonaquist paid for their residences. Although Moretti, Han Li, and Jehona fell head over heels in love with the property, they had to walk away because they didn't have the down payment. Unbeknownst to them, Cray told President Ballinger about their situation, and he told President Liu. Later that day, the two presidents stepped in and wired equal amounts of money from their personal bank accounts to cover the purchase price in appreciation for Moretti and Han Li saving their lives in Mongolia.

They moved into their new home exactly one year ago. In that year, three things happened. After Jehona graduated from middle school, she presented her parents with a brochure that one of her classmates gave her for a boarding school in Virginia. She said leaving the nest would give her greater self-confidence because it would force her to address the daily issues of life on her own. This was an about-face from her past position on boarding schools. Therefore, the brochure came as a complete surprise. However, their daughter also had a grasp on reality, saying she understood the cost involved and it was alright if she attended school locally.

The second thing which occurred was Cray telling his two operatives that they sucked at desk jobs and, in the past year, alienated many of those they needed to interact with because of their impatience and "my way or the highway" attitude. The words concession and compromise were in neither's vocabulary.

The third was that neither Cray, President Ballinger, nor President Liu could find suitable replacements for them after an intense look at hundreds of potential candidates. Being short two operatives, Nemesis was only semi-operational, which sidelined it from more complex missions. Cray and both presidents later admitted that they'd placed Moretti and Han Li on such high pedestals that only God was an acceptable replacement.

It also became apparent during their absence that; besides their field skills, they were the glue that held the team together. They projected to the other members the confidence that led everyone to believe they could accomplish the impossible. Cray told them they were at a career fork in the road. Either they had to quit Nemesis and get a job at another government agency that would tolerate their inability to work with others, which he said to his knowledge didn't exclude any government organization except Nemesis, or return as operatives. In response, Moretti and Han Li told him this was a family decision, and he would receive an answer within the week.

The following day, Moretti, Han Li, and Jehona drove to Virginia. It was the time of year when leaves were turning at the onset of winter, creating a sporadic pastel of colors in the landscape. The trio sat on a wooden bench in the boarding school's grassy courtyard with their daughter about to leave for an orientation class. She wasn't nervous. Her parents were. Not because she was leaving home, but because the day of reckoning had arrived to decide in response to Cray's ultimatum. Both were resolute in abiding with their daughter's wishes.

"Jehona, your mother and I need to make a decision, and we want your help," Moretti started out. "We've explained about Nemesis and what we did for a living. For the past year, we've had desk jobs. It hasn't gone like we'd hoped. Those positions are no longer available to us. Because of that, we need to decide if we leave Nemesis and find a desk job at another government agency, so we come home every night after work, or return to being operatives - which means traveling at a moment's notice into extremely perilous situations. A third option is for one of us to take a day job while the other goes back into the field."

Jehona started to reply, but Han Li held up her hand before she could speak.

"What your father and I would do as operatives is dangerous. If we returned to our previous positions, there is always a possibility something bad may happen to one or both of us. If it's both, you'll be placed into foster care until the age of 18. That's a major concern."

The teenager, who'd grown to five feet, seven inches tall, transforming from an anorexic-looking 90 pounds to 135, remained silent for a few seconds before responding.

"We're a family. Your happiness means as much to me as mine does to you. You bring justice to the world, helping people like me who cannot defend themselves. Besides, you're so unhappy when you return from work. I've almost told you several times to go back to your old jobs. If you don't help others because you're worried about me, that's guilt I can't carry for the rest of my life."

"Spoken like an adult who cares for her parents. But your mother mentioned a reality you can't ignore. You know how dangerous our job can be. You've experienced it firsthand. We're not immortal."

"You told me that if you live your life in fear of what could be, you'll never know what might have been."

"I said that," Moretti admitted. "Are you sure that you're only fifteen?"

"Uncle Jack, Uncle Doug, and Uncle John have given me their cell numbers in case I need help," she said, referring to Bonaquist, Cray, and the President of the United States. "They've promised to look in on me from time to time. Uncle John sent this in case I need help immediately. All I do is press this red button," Jehona said, pulling the red button with a clear plastic protector cap from her pocket.

"I guess we won't have to worry about you when we're gone. If you're OK with the risks, so are we."

After giving her parents a hug and a kiss on the cheek, Jehona looked at her Apple watch and said it was time for her to get to orientation. Not wanting to prolong the goodbye, she went into a slow run towards the building behind them.

CHAPTER 14

BURGAS IS A Bulgarian city of around 200,000 on the Black Sea. Located 15 miles north of it and visible only from the water was an abandoned Soviet submarine base constructed beneath a 3,000-acre hill - a craggy rock formation sprinkled with enough dirt to grow dense vegetation but agriculturally unsuited to produce anything of commercial value. It was the highest point in the area. Atop it was a four-story drab gray rectangular concrete structure with a sign indicating it was an oceanographic institute. Like many Soviet buildings, it was solidly built and architecturally brain-dead. While it was under construction, soviet military engineers secretly built the submarine base. Western intelligence agencies didn't have an inkling of its existence. When completed in 1983, the Soviet navy used it to send submarines on patrol and clandestinely insert special ops forces throughout the region.

The area atop the hill was deceptively dangerous. Thick with an undulating brush, beneath it were deep fissures that fell 1,500 feet to the Black Sea. More than one Soviet construction worker met their end by finding a fissure that the survey team missed. Steep jagged cliffs formed three sides of the hill - the fourth was a land bridge that connected to neighboring land. The base of the cliffs was littered with derelict boulders and rocks that Soviet engineers discarded rather than truck away and provide a clue to the extent of their construction activities. A narrow strip of sand that could hardly be called a beach was between this refuse and the Black Sea. The entrance to two submarine pens was through a natural crease, which some might refer to as a gap, at the base of a cliff. Soviet engineers dredged a deceptively deep channel that allowed their submarines to remain submerged as it passed through the crease - the dredging integrating seamlessly with that needed for the piers. From the water, the crease was one of many along the coast of the Black Sea. Two vertical lift elevators went from the submarine facility's interior, through the hill, and into the drab gray building. A second access to the building was by two slant elevators. These ran from the two piers, which protruded 200 feet into the sea, to the structure.

If not arriving by sea, access to the building was by a two-mile-long unmarked dirt road with a staffed gate that discouraged intrusion by the uninvited. This entrance was a red herring. The primary method for secretly getting people and equipment onto the property was through a three-mile-long tunnel with an unobtrusive entrance.

The naval base was abandoned with the fall of the Soviet Union and fell into disrepair. The newly established Russian Federation sold the property to the city of Burgas for $1 - although they neglected to mention that the site was a former military installation for fear that the city might believe that the Soviets dumped or spilled toxic and non-biodegradable chemicals on it - which they did.

Eagar to repatriate the land and eschewing an inspection of the property before the sale because the Russians wanted it that way, the city purchased it although they had no use for the land or derelict building. They just wanted to get their property back. The discovery of the submarine pens, which should have been surprising, wasn't. Burgas' residents always suspected the Soviets were hiding something, and this was confirmation of that deceit. Living in denial, city officials avoided sampling the soil for fear of what they'd find, which could lead to expensive remediation. Therefore, they looked for a buyer on whom to foist their problems, but who would pay the hefty property taxes that went along with such a large chunk of land - something the Soviets never did.

It took nearly three decades to find someone interested in purchasing a derelict drab gray building constructed by the Soviets and in need of extensive maintenance. The city sold it for what they paid the Russians - $1 but valued the property for tax purposes at $50 million. Rumor had it the purchaser was a wealthy Greek recluse because the person overseeing the structure's transformation on behalf of the buyer was that nationality. It was further surmised that the buyer liked their privacy, because of the property's isolated location, and wanted to live in anonymity.

Whoever the owner, everyone agreed they were serious about being left alone because they re-instituted the strict security employed by the Soviets, who were paranoid by nature, and expanded upon it by adding thermographic cameras which kept every square foot of the hill under surveillance. Unfortunately, the locals discovered the expanded security when several trespassed on the property and were met by a zealous security force who sent them to the hospital in an ambulance. Word got around, and they assiduously avoided the area.

Behar Tosku stood in front of his residence's thirty-foot-high glass windows that looked out to the Black Sea and sipped tsipouro, a strong distilled spirit from Crete that was 45 percent alcohol by volume and produced from the pomace, or residue of a wine press. Today was the anniversary of fleeing his compound in Rafina. He recalled how, following the Greek government's assault, he and Manjani took the boat anchored at the base of the cliff to a safe house in the village of Styra on the island of Euboea, which was less than 30 miles away. He was later told by informants that the government confiscated his assets because of information in a computer hard drive. They also said the Greek government and Interpol were searching for those abducted, police knocking on his now-former clients and intermediaries' doors.

Tosku took a deep breath and rubbed his eyes. The reflection on the past angered him because everything that happened a year ago was preventable if Moretti and Han Li were killed earlier. Many of his former clients went to jail because of the records on his computer. Not that he cared whether they spent the rest of their lives in a cell. What bothered him at the time was that he became highly radioactive - about to be investigated by more governments than he could count and all but certain to be hunted by contractors his clients hired to bury him along with what he knew. That he was alive a year later was an acknowledgment of how well he had obfuscated his whereabouts.

Tosku took a longer sip of the potent spirit, which he'd kept in the freezer to tone down its harshness. Continuing to look at the Black Sea, he thought about the choices he'd made in the past year. It began with deciding whether to retire, even though he technically was, because he had neither the clients nor the inventory or to go back into the same business.

That decision was made his third night in Styra. He'd gotten rich in human trafficking and illicit arms sales. Both industries were monetarily larger than the drug trade, the former generating annual global revenues of $32 billion with the latter $60 billion. Since he knew how to get and move inventory and who the buyers were for his merchandise, he decided to give it another go, this time operating from a country where he would be anonymous to his former clientele.

Tosku drained the shot glass of tsipouro and thought back to how he selected Bulgaria. He recalled that it was because of his past dealings in the Balkans where he noticed that the people were less curious and more accepting than the Greeks, possibly because of decades of Soviet occupation where survival trumped curiosity. Living there, he reasoned, would have the added benefit of being near merchandise - both people and weapons.

Once he decided on Bulgaria, an internet search found the property in Burgas. After sending Manjani to tour the site and reviewing the videos, a local law firm negotiated and closed the deal.

Ambassador Pullen sat at his desk and looked at a recording on his computer screen of Behar Tosku gazing at the Black Sea through the heavily tinted windows of what appeared to be his residence, judging from the furnishings behind him. The screen's date and legend showed that the video was taken ten days ago by a Sentinel drone.

President Ballinger sent the recording, along with a message that said two people would arrive within the next hour to give him a classified briefing on what he saw. Pullen phoned the front gate and told the marine in charge to expect the two individuals from Washington but didn't elaborate because he couldn't, not knowing their names or who they worked for. He assumed that they had the creds to get past the front gate and into the embassy compound if the president sent them.

Forty minutes later, they arrived and showed their creds to the guard who escorted them into the newly constructed building where the ambassador's office was located. Pullen's administrative assistant, knowing their identity, smiled and released the electronic door lock.

When the door opened, the ambassador did a doubletake. "I thought you both were dead," he said, getting up from his chair and going to put his arms around Moretti and Han Li. "What's it been, a year?"

"A little more," Moretti answered.

"President Ballinger never told me you were alive. The question is: how? Witnesses saw you, moments before the explosion, running down the steps to your room, which was disintegrated moments later."

Moretti explained that, when they registered at the Mystique, and after Han Li and Jehona left the reception desk, he asked the manager to put them in another room, but not change the number in their computer system or tell the staff. As the hotel wasn't full and wouldn't be for another week, she didn't have an issue with the request and handed him another key while allowing the room he was initially assigned to remain vacant. She told him the new room was at the opposite end of the hotel. He also asked her to list the occupant of the other room as Matthew Grogan.

"Smart. What made you do it?"

"To prevent one of the office staff from giving our room number to one of Tosku's contacts, even though the manager had a Greek name in the computer for that room."

"The two of you are alive because of that paranoia. But you were seen going down the steps to the room you were initially given."

"The stairway splits a third of the way down. You can't see that from above. Go left, and you head straight to our new room. It's about the same distance."

"Too bad you couldn't go straight to the airport. I sent a helicopter."

"We needed to go back and retrieve the flash drive," Han Li said. "The only thing we didn't expect was Jehona being taken while she waited for us."

"Thankfully, it worked out."

"Because of you," Moretti said. "If you hadn't convinced the prime minister to attack Tosku's compound, she'd be dead."

"Obviously, you retrieved the flash drive and somehow had the navy get it to me. Without it, I'm not sure the prime minister would have acted. Why did you both remain dead for a year?"

"Personal issues."

"Your daughter?"

"That was one. There were others."

"How did you get off Santorini undetected?"

"Following the explosion and Jehona being taken, we called the president. He dispatched a helicopter from the Naval Support Activity at Souda Bay in Crete to get us," Moretti replied. "The US military then transported us to the states. We didn't want to leave without Jehona, but President Ballinger promised you'd do whatever it took to get her back and that our staying would complicate that effort."

"He felt it was better if everyone believed you were dead. That way, they couldn't question you."

"That's about the size of it. We told him about the flash drive and believed that at least part of Tosku's operation was on it. The president ordered the navy to get it to you as quickly as possible."

"Which explains the naval officer. Speaking of Jehona, how is she?"

"Jehona Elira Moretti, our adopted daughter," Han Li answered, "has grown two inches since you last saw her and started high school. She's now five-feet, seven-inches tall."

"Congratulations."

"I'm sure you have questions about the video the president sent," Han Li said.

"How did you find him?"

"The two techs who work with us found Tosku," Han Li answered. She didn't mention that they were Kyle Alexson and Mike Connelly, both formerly with the NSA.

"My embassy techs help me with MS Word, while yours find Tosku," Pullen responded, his tone and facial expression showing that he didn't believe the techs Han Li spoke about were your average computer geeks any more than he thought they were bean counters.

Moretti continued where Han Li left off, with a hint of a smile on his face. "They're a little better than average. They traced a wire transfer from one of Tosku's banks in Crete to a bank in Burgas, Bulgaria - although neither account was in his name. I'd explain the details, but I don't understand the half of it, although I believe it had something to do with that bank being the one who issued the captain of the *Hercules* a credit card, which he used for fuel and sundries."

"I thought he was smarter than that."

"He may not have wanted to spook the local bank with wiring money from a numbered offshore account. That reeks of drug money. I'm sure he didn't want that rumor attached to him because it gets the government's attention. He figured his alias and that the bank was in Bulgaria was adequate to hide his new identity."

"How did you find his residence?"

"The techs hacked the bank's server."

"These techs wouldn't have an employment history that involves one or more of the alphabet agencies?"

"Let's stay away from that subject."

Pullen changed gears. "The residence looks impressive and expensive."

"It belonged to the Soviets who used it as a secret submarine base. We pulled from the city of Burgas computer system the architectural, engineering, electrical, water, and other pertinent drawings for the residence."

"I assume the reason you're here is to punch his ticket."

"We're here to ensure his trafficking days are over," Moretti answered. "How that happens is up to Han Li and me."

"I would expect a SEAL team instead of you two."

"That's a reasonable assumption since Tosku sent two missiles into the embassy compound. Han Li and I wanted to handle this because it's personal, especially what they did to Jehona and killing Defrim Kote."

"And to protect your daughter, should Tosku decide to send someone to the US to even the score."

"Another reason the president gave us the green light."

"What you told me is interesting, but it doesn't explain why you came to see me. The embassy has video conferencing."

"We need an aluminum briefcase and a ride."

"Where?"

"They told him"

"Why?"

"They also told him."

"This ought to be interesting," Pullen said.

The NAS helicopter from Souda Bay, which Ambassador Pullen summoned to transport a diplomatic courier package and its two escorts, landed in the embassy's courtyard and kept its rotors turning as the man carrying the aluminum briefcase and the attractive woman beside him climbed onboard. Lifting off, it headed for the Aegean Sea.

The briefcase, which was tightly bound by a metal strap with a numbered metal plate, had a courier tag that identified the recipient as the President of the United States. However, instead of sensitive documents, it contained a bottle of Crown Royal Reserve - President Ballinger's favorite alcoholic beverage. The contents of the briefcase, however, weren't important. This was a way for Moretti and Han Li to plausibly go to a specific US military installation without revealing their identity. Since it was routine to send diplomatic pouches to military airbases, from which they were securely routed to their destinations, posing as couriers were the perfect cover to get them where they needed to go without arousing suspicion.

Lieutenant Colonel Cray, the head of the president's Statistical Analysis Division and the administrative commander of Nemesis, coordinated with the Pentagon to provide Moretti and Han Li's next mode of transport once they arrived on base. He didn't tell his contact at the Department of Defense why he needed the aircraft and gear, only that he had two individuals who required a C-130, and they'd give the pilot the coordinates for their high-altitude parachute jump. Since no one was about to turn down a request from someone associated with the White House, the aircraft and gear were quickly approved, and orders were sent to the referenced military base parroting what Cray said. Classified military operations were a way of life in the Pentagon, and once this order was forwarded, it was overshadowed by other urgencies and quickly forgotten.

"It's done," Cray said, turning to the president who was in the Treaty Room on the second floor of the residence, which he frequently used as a study. Putting his cell phone in his pocket, Cray took a seat in the thickly padded club chair next to him.

"I know I said this can't be a Nemesis operation since it doesn't directly impact the security of either the United States or China, but it's damn hard not sending the rest of the team to join them and eliminate a son of a bitch who's destroyed and continues to destroy the lives of so many children," Ballinger said.

"It's the right call, sir. Anything more than the support we're providing risks exposure. It's hard enough keeping this unit a secret as it is."

Ballinger ran his hands through his hair, his dissatisfaction with the situation apparent from the sour expression on his face. "I let them talk me into having them do this, knowing they'd have one arm tied behind their backs. I admire them, Doug. They're a combination of the Equalizer, the Punisher, and the Transporter." Ballinger was addicted to movies where someone, legally or not, balanced the scales of justice and helped those who couldn't defend themselves. "Once the bad guys are in their sights," he continued, "nothing short of death that will keep them from succeeding. They have the moral high ground in what they're attempting, and I'm sitting on my ass wishing them well. That's hot air with nothing behind it. You'd think I was still in Congress."

Cray remained silent.

The president took a deep breath and leaned back in his chair for nearly a minute with a pensive look on his face. "Maybe I can put my thumb on the scales of justice. Here's what I want you to do."

CHAPTER 15

THE HELICOPTER LANDED at Bezmer Air Base near the Bulgarian city of Yambol, a joint United States-Bulgarian airfield 58 miles directly west of Burgas that the US military viewed as one of its six critical overseas airbases. Moretti and Han Li, who were not on the helicopter's manifest, left the aircraft, and Moretti turned over the aluminum briefcase to the base administrative officer who met them.

They drove, per the instructions the officer received from the Pentagon, to a hangar where a C-130 was parked. The crew was told to expect a man and a woman who would conduct a high-altitude, high-opening, or HAHO, jump over a location they would provide once onboard. Not knowing their destination ahead of time wasn't unusual; the aircrew was used to it, having inserted more than a few nameless special ops and intelligence agency types - although none as beautiful as the woman who stepped out of the administrative officer's vehicle.

The crew chief greeted his nameless passengers and took them on board. He didn't request an ID because operatives parachuting uninvited to wherever they were going didn't carry one. That the base administrative officer escorted them, and the aircrew received orders from Washington to expect the man and the woman, was the only authentication needed.

Once on the aircraft, Moretti went to the cockpit and greeted the two pilots, handing the pilot in command a folded piece of paper containing the drop coordinates he'd received from Cray. "This is where you're going to let us off the bus," Moretti said.

The pilot unfolded the paper and, giving him a surprised look, removed a chart from the flight bag behind his seat. Putting his finger on their destination, he turned the chart so the co-pilot could see.

"Since you're making a HAHO jump 58 miles from here," the pilot in command stated, "I assume it's because you don't want anyone on the ground to hear the aircraft or your parachutes opening, which they would with a low-altitude jump."

"You have it."

"If either of you haven't done this type of parachuting before, the jumpmaster can answer your questions. Once you leap out of this aircraft, it's going to be difficult to raise your hand and ask."

"We've both been to Yuma."

The pilot nodded, showing that he knew Moretti referred to the military free fall facility at the JFK Special Warfare Center and School at the Yuma Proving Grounds in Arizona. What Moretti didn't say was that every operative in Nemesis went to that school and, for an ex-Army Ranger who'd been there before, it was a refresher class.

Moretti returned to the rear of the aircraft and was approached by the jumpmaster. "Let's get you both geared up," he said. "The orders I received gave your heights and weights. The high-altitude exposure suits are on the webbed seats behind you. They're certified for temperatures as low as -76 degrees Fahrenheit. You'll be exiting the aircraft at 25,000 feet, where the temp will be -30. Your tactical gear is in those two bags," he said, pointing to them. After you put on your gear, I'll help get you into your suits."

They changed from their civilian clothes into Crye G3 combat pants and shirt, over which they put a JPC armor vest. For their footwear, Cray provided Bates 922 boots, a favorite with the SEAL teams. Although Han Li wasn't the least bit shy about stripping down and getting changed, the jumpmaster looked the other way as she donned her tactical gear. Once on, he helped them into the exposure suits, designed so that the inside front and the arms had thermal insulation, allowing the body to remain cool during long pre-breathes. After binding the Velcro cuffs on their ankles and wrists, he handed them what special operators referred to as a Bunny Helmet - a leather ballistic helmet with communication, oxygen, and night vision goggle attachments. After securing the collar on their exposure suits, he summoned the physiology technician waiting in the hangar. She came on board as they were putting on their helmets.

The tech introduced herself and told Moretti and Han Li to sit in the webbed seats behind them. "Let's get you hooked up," she said, taking the lines that were connected to the two yellow oxygen tanks beneath their seats and attaching them to their Bunny Helmets. Turning a valve on each tank to start the flow, she told Moretti and Han Li to secure their masks. They did.

"You know the drill. You'll pre-breathe 100 percent oxygen for 45 minutes to flush nitrogen from your bloodstream. Once that's done, I'll disconnect the oxygen line you're on," she said, tugging gently on the one running from the tank beneath Han Li's seat to illustrate, "and replace it with the one from your internal oxygen tank."

Moretti and Han Li gave a thumbs up.

As the tech sat in a webbed seat on the other side of the aircraft to observe them, the jumpmaster approached. "You already know what I'm about to tell you, but I'm going to repeat it to refresh your memories. You'll jump at 25,000 feet. Ten seconds later, deploy your parachutes. Use the GPS embedded in your suits to guide you to your target. While you're pre-breathing, I'll enter the coordinates you gave the pilot."

Forty-five minutes later, the physiology tech looked at his watch and, standing in front of Moretti and Han Li, performed a couple of tests to confirm their lucidness. Afterward, she told the jumpmaster they were good to go. The aircraft took off 15 minutes later.

The C-130 was climbing to its 25,000-foot target altitude when the jumpmaster heard the co-pilot telling him through his headset that they were 20 minutes from the drop zone. The red light next to the rear cargo door went on. Ten minutes later, with the aircraft level at altitude and speeding along at 210 mph, the jumpmaster told his two passengers to get ready. Nine minutes later, he held up his index finger - a visual cue they were one minute from the drop zone. Moretti and Han Li started toward the rear of the aircraft as the cargo door opened.

Having a common rate of descent is critical in keeping the team together so that everyone arrives at the target simultaneously, with their glide slopes ideally being as uniform as possible. Therefore, Moretti and Han needed to be roughly the same weight when they left the aircraft.

That meant the ex-Army Ranger, who tipped the scales eighty pounds heavier than the statuesque brunette, didn't parachute with the equipment container, which was packed with enough mission essentials to equalize their weights.

Through the speakers in their Bunny Helmets, Moretti and Han Li heard the pilot counting down the seconds to the jump point. Once that number reached zero, the red light went out, and a green light appeared. An instant later, they leaped in tandem into the black void.

The C-130 drop point was 30 miles from Tosku's residence. Guided by their GPS monitors and their night vision goggles, they saw their target and deployed their RA-1 parachutes at 5,000 feet. Both landed on the roof of the building within two seconds of each other, Han Li touching down a little harder than she wanted because of the eighty pounds of equipment she carried. They let out a sigh of relief when there wasn't an armed response nor the sound of a klaxon to their incursion.

After removing their exposure suits, they reached into the equipment container and replaced their Bunny Helmets with a black Crye Nightcap, reattaching their communications link and night vision goggles to it. The weapons were next - arming themselves with holstered silenced Heckler & Koch MK 23 SOCOM pistols, which they fastened to their right leg, and an MK 17 assault rifle, which they slung across their chests. Each then grabbed a block of C-4 explosive, a detonator, and a thin nylon rope. Han Li took the black box, which transmitted a single frequency that would ignite both detonators.

Moretti went to the side of the roof that faced away from the sea and paced off six feet from the left corner. Inserting the detonator into the C-4, he lowered it with the nylon rope to the ground. Han Li lowered her charge onto a large steel box 20 feet from the opposite corner of the building.

The rappelling gear was next. They put on their harnesses and gloves before lifting their backpacks from the container, which had spare ammo and other essentials needed to enter the building.

"Ready when you are," Moretti said, attaching his carabiner to the steel safety rail which ringed the roof.

Han Li did the same.

They simultaneously threw their X-Stand Safe Climb Ropes over the side. This safety system used a Prusik knot that slid up and down the climbing rope and cinched tight if a fall occurred. Getting into position, they stepped off the edge and started down the side of the building.

The reason for rappelling and not picking the lock or busting through the roof access door was Karas's report. It stated that Tosku's Rafina compound employed an extensive system of thermographic cameras, klaxons, and door sensors. Therefore, while they believed they could unobtrusively land on the roof, it was questionable whether entering the residence through the roof door might trigger an alarm. They didn't want to get caught on top of the building with nowhere to go. The method by which they planned to enter the residence was only marginally better, which was cutting an entry hole in one of the windows that faced the Black Sea. Since it was apparent these tall windows couldn't be opened, it was unlikely they'd have a security sensor on or near them. Or so they believed.

Thirty feet below the roof, at the bottom of one of the large window panels that comprised the building's sea-facing wall, Moretti reached into his backpack, removed a carbide-tipped glass cutter, and scored a large rectangle. He next applied equal pressure with both hands and attempted to break the cut section free. When nothing happened, Han Li joined in. However, it quickly became apparent that the rectangle wasn't going anywhere. Han Li told Moretti to stop trying and to move to the side. Without saying another word, she brought her right leg back and kicked the center of the rectangle. It broke free and fell onto the carpeted floor.

They entered the residence. Immediately, a klaxon sounded, and every light in the room came on. Nearly blinded by the sudden burst of brightness, they flipped up their NVG's as the security staff poured into the room.

Diving behind a setting of two thick chairs and a couch, which absorbed the bullets flying in their direction, they returned fire with their MK 17's. In that exchange, the wall of glass behind them shattered and disappeared. The three pieces of heavy furniture protecting them were quickly being chewed up from the relentless gunfire. It was clear Tosku had more than enough men to fend them off, and there was no way they could fight their way into the residence and capture or kill him. They'd be fortunate to survive.

"Let's get out of here," Moretti said.

Han Li didn't reply. Instead, since she and Moretti had their rappelling gear still attached, she untied her Prusik knot and leaped through the opening where the floor-to-ceiling windows had been. Moretti did the same and was inches behind - each controlling their fall with their gloves. Since the ropes weren't long enough to get them to the surface, they disconnected from them seven feet above the ground and fell hard onto it. They took cover in back of the boulders several feet away, bullets ricocheting off the boulders and piercing the surface of the Black Sea behind them. They were boxed in. If they believed things couldn't get any worse, they were wrong. Looking up, they saw the two slant passenger elevators descending towards the piers next to them - their lighted interiors showing that each was packed with security guards.

"Now would be a good time to set off the detonators," Moretti said.

Han Li removed the remote-control transmitter from her pocket, threw up the plastic safety cover, and pressed the button. There were two simultaneous explosions. One cut the primary power, and the second destroyed the backup generator. The slant elevators stopped a quarter of the way to the piers, and their interiors went dark.

"Tosku's security will be in disarray in this darkness. Let's go back to the residence and get him," Moretti said.

"That works. I'll tell our ride it's taking longer than expected," Han Li responded and made the call on the handheld she removed from her backpack.

While this was happening, the guards inside the elevator seemed to have gotten an epiphany that they weren't completely helpless and broke the elevator's glass windows. They began firing indiscriminately in the direction where they'd last seen the intruders. However, with neither NVG's nor a reference point, their bullets never came close to Moretti or Han Li.

"The only way to enter the building without going to the top of this hill is through the sub pens," Han Li said. "The architectural drawings show there's an interior stairway next to the elevators."

"Tosku will have an escape plan, just as he did in Rafina. We can surprise him if we hurry."

It wouldn't be long before Moretti would need to change that statement.

CHAPTER 16

NEITHER BEHAR TOSKU nor Taulant Manjani slept in what most in Burgas referred to as "the residence," which was the enormous building atop the hill that overlooked the Black Sea. Instead, they slept in a spacious and luxurious panic room that was engineered to be impervious to physical, gas, and biological attacks. Its interior was enormous, measuring 120 feet to a side with a ten-foot-high ceiling. Stored within it was enough food to last six months and access to a large freshwater reservoir in an adjoining fortified area. The reservoir's water had an extensive filtering process that extracted foreign substances and organisms as small as a virus. Also within this enclosure was a security console that accessed every camera on the property and a hardened cable internet link connected to a hidden satellite dish two miles away.

The panic room and part of the submarine pen had a power source and backup generator separate from the residence. Contractors brought in by Manjani from other southeastern European countries installed both following a secret renovation. Trucks transported the equipment and materials needed for the construction and entered through the secret tunnel that transected the hill. Construction took six months, with workers led to believe this was a secret government project which couldn't be discussed with family members.

Both Tosku and Manjani were asleep when the klaxon sounded. They awoke, hearts pounding, and went to the security console to see what triggered the alarm. Uniformly, both were incredulous when they saw Moretti and Han Li. Incredulity turned to anger, seeing them escape by rappelling from the residence. That mood didn't improve upon hearing the explosions that shook the panic room, followed by the property going dark.

"Many of our guards are on the elevators," Manjani said, pointing to the heavy gunfire coming from each.

"Why aren't they dead?" Tosku vented.

Manjani didn't reply.

"More importantly, how did they find me? If they did, so could others. I need to know."

Manjani remained silent, unable to answer the unexplainable.

"They'll have to come in here. It's the only way off the rocky area they're in."

"How do you want to handle it?"

Tosku told him.

As they entered the submarine pens, Moretti stopped and looked around. "I'm surprised there's no security."

"There's quite a few guards in the slant elevators. Whoever's left wouldn't think that we'd return to the residence. Who'd be crazy enough to do that?"

"Us. Which should be a significant notation on our future psych evals if we survive," Moretti said as they continued inside.

Two-thirds of the way into the cavernous space, they heard a popping sound coming from above. Looking up, they saw a cluster of round metal-like objects dropping from the ceiling. As each struck the concrete floor, it burst into a cloud of white gas. Holding their breath, they ran towards the exit just as several thick interlocking metal panels dropped from above and sealed it. Unable to hold their breath any longer, each involuntarily gasped. Seconds later, they collapsed.

Once the interlocking metal panels retracted and the gas vented, Tosku and Manjani approached the unconscious figures.

"Unfold a couple of tables and bind each to one. I have some questions for our zealous pursuers."

Manjani brought two eight-foot-long rectangular folding metal tables, stored in the corner of the submarine pens, and set them up. He also carried four rolls of duct tape. After lifting Moretti and Han Li onto the tables, he secured them with duct tape. Leaving Tosku alone, Manjani took the interior stairway to his office and returned with his interrogation kit. Looking at the two with whom he was about to have an intimate conversation, he saw they'd regained consciousness, and Tosku was speaking to them.

"You've cost me, as best as I can estimate, around $400,000,000," Tosku said, looking down at his captives. "If I'm forced to leave Burgas, you can add another $50,000,000. For what? The girl's an orphan. A nobody. She and her kind are leeches sucking money and resources from those who contribute to society."

"That's rich coming from the biggest bloodsucker of all. What do you contribute to society?" Moretti asked. "Nothing. You live a luxurious lifestyle, while those you traffic in are virtually slaves. You make me want to puke. On you, of course."

As Moretti was speaking, he and Han Li were looking at Tosku. Neither saw Manjani pick up an ice pick from his interrogation kit and jab it into the palm of the ex-Ranger. The cry of pain that followed elicited a smile from Tosku and his interrogator.

"Mr. Manjani, please start your questioning with the pretty lady," Tosku said, then watched as the interrogator pulled the ice pick from Moretti's palm and went back to his interrogation kit and exchanged it for a scalpel.

Manjani held the scalpel over Han Li's right cheek. "This is how it works," he said. "I ask a question, and you reply. If I consider your answer honest, nothing happens. If it's the opposite or incomplete, a subjective decision, I'll cut you. First question. Tell me how you learned we were here."

The look that Han Li gave him was defiant and communicated her unwillingness to talk. Then her expression rapidly transformed from defiant to one of confusion and finally comprehension, understanding what was about to happen when she saw the red dot in the center of his forehead. An instant later, the red dot was replaced by a jagged hole. His body was hurled backward and landed several feet away on the concrete floor, his eyes staring blankly at the ceiling. Tosku made a beeline for his panic room but never got there. A bullet found the upper part of his right leg after he'd taken three steps, and he fell to the ground screaming in pain.

"I think it's time we get you both out of here," Bonaquist said, entering the submarine pen with two other members of Nemesis - Yan He and Blaine McGough. Jack Bonaquist, a former member of the president's Secret Service detail, took out his 8.25" USMC spring-assisted folding knife and cut Moretti and Han Li free while McGough, a former force recon marine and the newest team member, went to Tosku. Yan He, a lieutenant colonel in China's PLA, said he'd search the submarine pen's interior to ensure none of Tosku's men were hiding inside.

The human trafficker was crying in pain as McGough approached. Removing a pair of flex restraints from a pocket in his vest, he placed one over Tosku's wrists and the other above the wound, cinching both and causing him to scream.

"Shut up, you're giving me a headache," McGough said as he retrieved the roll of duct tape off the floor, ripped off a couple of long strips, and tightly wrapped them over the trafficker's wound. Grabbing Tosku by his collar, he dragged him along the floor to where Moretti and Han Li were standing.

"I'm wounded, you cretin. Give me something for the pain," Tosku shouted.

"I can do that," McGough replied, bending down and punching him hard between the eyes and rendering him unconscious. "Do you still want this asshole as a prisoner?" he asked Bonaquist as he put Tosku in a firefighter's carry. "If you don't, I'll give him a crash course in drown proofing. He'll fail"

"Ask him," Bonaquist said, pointing to Moretti.

"He'll be coming with us. I have something else in mind."

"Have it your way," McGough responded as he left the enclosure with Tosku draped over his shoulders.

Once the former marine left, Han Li asked Bonaquist if he encountered resistance from Tosku's security force.

"None. The Sentinel saw everyone who wasn't stranded in the slant elevators," he responded with a grin, "leaving the area in a hurry. It might have something to do with a large submarine close to shore with the US flag illuminated atop its mast. They might have gotten the impression that a special forces team was coming ashore and didn't want any part of that."

"How are we going to explain an American sub in Bulgarian water?" Han Li asked.

"Explain it to who? The good citizens of Burgas can't see this cove unless they're on top of it."

"The security guards saw it."

"Who's going to believe them? Whatever they say, we'll deny."

"Let's back up," Moretti said. "How and why are you here? Getting rid of Tosku has nothing to do with Nemesis."

"The president ordered us to protect you. He felt Nemesis would be severely impacted if it lost its two top operatives. We can talk about this later. We have to go," Bonaquist said with a note of urgency.

"Before we do, we need to search the building to get computers and anything else that might reveal Tosku's new business activities."

"Good idea. You'll also want to retrieve your gear from the roof."

"You saw that?" Moretti asked.

"I saw the live feed from the Sentinel while we were aboard *Ohio*. Let's move it. Daylight is 45 minutes away."

Although Moretti was the operational commander and team leader of Nemesis and would typically make these decisions, he was the one being rescued and Bonaquist called the shots.

The acting team leader split his team - Yan He would search the panic room, while everyone else, except for

McGough, who was on his way to the RIB with Tosku, searched the residence.

Seeing there was a biometric reader at the entrance to the panic room, Yan He removed a breaching charge from his backpack and blew the door off its supports. Entering the enclosure, he grabbed two laptops and the hard drive from the server before leaving. There was nothing else of significance within. At the same time, Moretti and Han Li retrieved their equipment container and put everything, including the exposure suits and parachutes, inside. Moretti dragged it down the stairs to the submarine pen, where he added the guns that Tosku had taken from them. He and Han Li were waiting to exfil when Bonaquist returned.

"We have a serious problem. Tosku was using his residence to house his trafficking victims. Two floors above us, there are over a hundred frightened children locked in cells. The question is: what do we do with them with daylight almost here?"

"If we cut them loose, they'll wander the hills trying to escape. Some will get injured or die," Han Li added.

"The safe play is to keep them in their cells and ensure they have adequate food and water. We'll send an anonymous message to the mayor and other public officials in Burgas informing them of the children," Moretti said. "Alexson and Connelly can send them a text or email. That'll be grade school simple for them."

Bonaquist and Han Li thought that suggestion made sense.

"The locals won't know what happened when they see the damage to the residence and a body with a hole in its head," Bonaquist said.

"They'll assume Tosku, or whatever alias he went by, was attacked by someone as unsavory as him and escaped and abandoned his captives."

"I like it. Let's make sure the children have enough food and water before we go to the sub."

Moretti, Han Li, Bonaquist, and Yan He went into the residence. Finding cases of water and packaged food, they brought them downstairs to where the children were imprisoned and passed it through the bars. Two of the captives spoke English, and Han Li explained that help was coming and that the person responsible for kidnapping and imprisoning them was in their custody. The two captives explained this in their native tongues to others who relayed it in their native languages and so forth. Eventually, everyone knew help was on the way. From their expressions, the fear that gripped them ratcheted down a notch or two.

The *USS Ohio* was a nuclear-powered fleet ballistic missile submarine, which was later converted to carry guided missiles. It was 560 feet long, had a beam of 42 feet, and a displacement of 18,750 metric tons. Crewed by 15 officers and 140 enlisted, it carried 154 Tomahawk cruise missiles that could be launched through its 22 vertical tubes. Besides being on patrol and waiting for orders to pound the United States' enemies with cruise missiles, *Ohio* conducted clandestine insertions and exfil operations. The submarine was on its way out of Bulgarian waters.

Once Moretti had the wound in his hand stitched, and he and Han Li got cleaned up, the Nemesis team assembled in the captain's cabin. Because it was small, everyone stood.

The captain handed Moretti an envelope stamped Top Secret / SCI, meaning it was sensitive compartmented information. Moretti read the single piece of paper inside, handed it to Bonaquist, who read it and handed it to Han Li - and so forth until every member of the team saw what was on the paper.

"Before I go into what the president sent," Bonaquist said to the captain, "can you tell the two members of our team we brought aboard your previous orders?"

The captain thought it was a good idea for everyone to be on the same page and gave Moretti and Han Li a summary of his received orders. "President Ballinger ordered *Ohio* to curtail its patrol and proceed to a rendezvous point where a helo would lower the three of you onto my deck," he said, looking at Bonaquist, McGough, and Yan He. "I was to then floor it to the coordinates we just left. The president indicated that he wanted *Ohio* to remain surfaced and as close to shore as possible. During this time, I was to show the flag and focus a bright light on it."

"That made you quite a target," Moretti said.

"It got everyone's blood pumping. My orders also said that I could only fire my weapons in self-defense to safeguard my vessel and crew. Once the team returned, they'd give me *Ohio*'s next destination."

"And you want to know where that is?" Bonaquist asked.

"It helps if I plot a course that avoids undersea listening devices, satellite surveillance areas, aerial patrols, and other subs. Stuff like that."

Everyone laughed, liking the captain's sense of humor.

Bonaquist pointed to Moretti.

"I spoke with the president twice - once on my way to *Ohio* and once on deck before it submerged."

"My communications officer didn't tell me."

Bonaquist removed the satphone from his pocket and held it up. The captain nodded, getting the inference.

"Because of what occurred in Burgas, there was a change in plans. That required not only coordination with a third party but also the use of one of their assets."

"Where are we going?" the captain asked, throwing the question to no one in particular.

"*Ohio* will rendezvous with another vessel in the Black Sea. Look at the first set of coordinates," Moretti said, handing the captain the paper on which he copied the coordinates the president read to him. "I can read my numbers if you have a problem. The RIB isn't the smoothest form of transport."

The captain looked at what he was handed. "You would have made a good doctor, but I can read it."

That elicited a smile from Moretti.

"This appears to be smack in the middle of the Black Sea," the captain said.

"I'm told we'll have to wait for approximately fourteen hours until the other vessel arrives," Moretti said. "When it does, you'll surface, and we'll transfer our prisoner. Afterward, you'll take us to the coordinates below where a helo will get us off your hands."

"I should mention," Bonaquist said. "if any of the crew knows the person who we carried on board, keep it to themselves. The same goes if they see a picture of him or any of us in the future."

"We've hauled our share of special operators and their detainees. The crew is well versed in OPSEC," he replied, referring to operations security.

"I would expect no less," Moretti said, complimenting the captain. "The rendezvous is sensitive. You'll be the only one permitted to look through the periscope. Our team will bring the prisoner topside and hand him over while the crew remains below deck. I would appreciate it if he could be sedated and placed on IVs before the transfer."

"That won't be a problem. What's the name of the vessel we're rendezvousing with?"

"The Changzheng 6. It's a Chinese submarine. I would appreciate it if you didn't blow it out of the water when it approaches."

CHAPTER 17

THE *CHANGZHENG 6* was a Chinese Xia class submarine that carried the JL-3 SLBM, a submarine-launched ballistic missile with a range of 4,600 miles. Its designated patrol area went from the Mediterranean Sea to the Arabian Sea. However, occasionally, it received orders to leave that area for a special operations mission, such as the one which the submarine's captain just received.

Following President Ballinger's call to President Liu, *Changzheng 6* was determined to be the closest Chinese sub to *Ohio*. Orders were issued and, fourteen hours later, the *SLBM* rose from the depths of the Black Sea a mile from the surfaced American submarine. The captains communicated with one another in English using marine VHF. When the Chinese sub stopped 50 yards from *Ohio,* its forward hatch was thrown open, and four sailors emerged - two of them carrying lines.

As *Changzheng 6* was approaching the American submarine, Bonaquist and Yan He brought the stretcher with a sedated Tosku on deck. With Moretti, Han Li, and McGough's help, they lowered it into the RIB. The five Nemesis operatives then took off with their prisoner towards the Chinese sub. The waters were calm as the RIB gently touched the side of the vessel. A crew member tossed a line to Moretti and another to McGough to secure the RIB. Once done, they lowered two additional lines, which McGough attached to the support at each end of the stretcher, which was lifted off the RIB and taken below deck. Moments later, the hatch closed.

There was no simple way to get Tosku to where he was going - a patch of land that bordered the Bohai Sea. Transporting him by air would have been a 4,313-mile flight - long, but faster and easier than putting him on a submarine. However, since his destination was a Chinese military installation, that came with insurmountable challenges. The first was the inability to land a foreign or unmarked aircraft there because it would invite too many unanswerable questions, such as what it was doing on a military base. Too many curious people meant the government would have to come up with answers - something to be avoided.

Conversely, putting Tosku's ass on a Chinese aircraft would in theory work since it could land on the military installation without raising suspicion. However, that created another problem - how to unobtrusively get him on that plane. Landing a Chinese aircraft in Burgas or a nearby city with an airfield would also invite unanswerable questions. Therefore, presidents Ballinger and Liu decided on an unobtrusive mode of transport - a Chinese submarine, avoiding the complexities of air transport.

While a sub would get Tosku to China without being seen, the nautical route to Bohai was anything but direct and significantly longer than the distance an aircraft would travel. *Changzheng 6* docked at the Lushun submarine base, a stone's throw from Dalian, two weeks and six hours after receiving its prisoner. Met by a white unmarked cargo van, two men from the sub placed a large black canvas bag in the rear. Inside was the sedated human trafficker, placed in the bag to hide him from a non-US recon satellite which kept Lushun under constant surveillance. It also removed the possibility that someone with a cell phone might take a picture of the prisoner being escorted to the van.

The van went to the Chou Shui Tze airbase in the northwestern part of the city where a Shaanxi Y-8, a medium-range transport aircraft, was waiting. Once aboard, he was taken out of the canvas bag, given an injection to counteract the sedative, and shackled to one of the steel seats at the rear of the aircraft.

The flight from the Chou Shui Tze airbase to the military airfield in Mohe, the northernmost city in China, was 1,251 miles. Once the pilot shut down the aircraft's engines and the crew chief opened the rear hatch, two PLA soldiers came aboard and, replacing the prisoner's shackles with those they carried, placed a black hood over Tosku's head and took him to their car.

It took 20 minutes to get to the black prison. When it arrived, the two guards pulled Tosku from the rear of the car and brought him to Colonel Leung Tao, the prison's commandant. President Liu recently promoted him two ranks for his performance in running the prison and his ability to keep what went on there a secret.

One of the guards removed the prisoner's black hood while the other kept a firm grip on his upper left arm.

As soon as Tosku saw the commandant, all the rage that was pent-up inside released. Speaking in English, which he believed to be the most common communicative language for conducting business, he laid out his demands. The first was to see the Greek ambassador. The second was to speak with a lawyer.

Leung, who rarely saw defiance from a prisoner because most were too scared to utter a word, turned around and picked up a two-foot-long bamboo baton from his desk. He jabbed the end into Tosku's midsection three times in rapid succession with a practiced motion. The human trafficker doubled over in pain and tried to drop to his knees but was jerked to his feet by the PLA officers beside him.

"Welcome to Mohe," Leung said in broken English. "This is the most remote and secure military prison in China, although it doesn't officially exist. You are prisoner number 41786. If you use anything but this number to identify yourself, you will be severely beaten. You're here until you die. When you do, we'll throw you in the furnace along with the rest of the garbage. I know what you're thinking-it's possible to escape from any prison. Not this one. Ignoring the military airfield, the nearest shelter is a town is 200 miles away. In the winter, where it regularly drops to -40 degrees Fahrenheit and some days lower, you will freeze, starve, or be eaten by wolves or bears. In the summer, anyone you encounter will gladly turn you in for a reward - the penalty for hiding you being death."

Tosku didn't appear intimidated, his facial expression displaying his skepticism that he was being told the entire truth.

"You have information that I've been ordered to get, starting with a detailed explanation of your trafficking and arms businesses and the names of everyone involved. Your interrogation will segue into other areas - which we'll get into later. I know what you're thinking: you have no intention of giving me what I want. Other men thought the same. None succeeded."

"I'll be the exception."

One of the guards was about to deliver a blow to Tosku's midsection, instilling in him he was to shut up when the commandant talked and to speak only when asked a question. Leung raised his right hand a fraction of an inch, stopping the guard.

"Rules. If you lie or try to keep information from us, you will be traumatized, taken back to your cell, and the process will repeat ad infinitum until I'm satisfied you've been truthful. If you're disruptive or disobey the guards, you'll be beaten, and your food taken away for one day. If you try and starve yourself, you will be force-fed until you recover and then beaten severely."

"I'll never tell you anything because, as soon as I do, I'll be killed. Eventually, I'll get free."

"Your freedom is gone. And you're wrong about me wanting to kill you. The person who I report to said that I couldn't. He and I share a personal repugnance for those who traffic in children. We believe there is no lower form of life. We've devised an innovative punishment for you. Do you know what one of the biggest disruptors in prison is?"

Tosku shook his head in the negative.

"Sexual tension. Even though prisoners are regularly tortured, it would surprise you at their proclivity to have sex with one another. It's not something we interfere with because it has a calming effect on the population."

"Why are you telling me this?" Tosku asked, maintaining his arrogant voice.

"Because I intend to let every prisoner in this facility, save for a few, continually have their way with you. Since you've allowed this to happen to countless children, you should have the same experience."

The commandant nodded to the guard, who punched the human trafficker in the solar plexus, picked him up off the floor, and hit him again in the exact location. Tosku collapsed, gasping for breath. The guards left him on the floor writhing in pain.

"Get up," Leung ordered.

Having lost his bravado, Tosku obeyed.

"Excellent. We'll begin your interrogation early, so you won't miss dinner. The sergeant," Leung said, pointing to the unsmiling man who'd just struck him, "has a procedure we perform on our new prisoners to get them in the right frame of mind. Not to worry, your fingernails will grow back."

CHAPTER 18

ETURNING FROM BULGARIA, Moretti and Han Li spent the next day sorting through their mail, cleaning the house, and restocking the refrigerator. On Friday, they got into their black four-door Ford F-150 at three in the morning for the six-hour drive to pick up Jehona for the weekend. On their way back, they stopped at her favorite restaurant, Go Greek, in a small strip center near their house. She feasted on her favorite meal of loukaniko with a side of Greek fries, while Han Li had the pork souvlaki and Moretti the lamb gyro. For an appetizer, they shared a plate of dolmades.

When they returned home, Han Li put the laundry their daughter brought with her in the washer, while Moretti and Jehona sat on the couch in the living room and talked. Following their conversation, Jehona gave him a big hug.

Moretti and Han Li usually began their day at five with a five-mile run, regardless of the weather. Following this, they would go into a spare bedroom, which they'd transformed into an exercise room, and work out for the next hour. Today, however, since Jehona was home, they got up at their usual time and sat in the kitchen, Moretti drinking coffee and Han Li green tea, waiting for their daughter to get up. An hour later, she came into the kitchen. Han Li dished up the steel-cut oatmeal she'd prepared earlier, topping it with a mound of blueberries. Jehona tore into it.

"I got a message from Cray," Moretti said, getting up from the table and handing his phone to Han Li so she could see the text. "The president is having a meet and greet at his residence late this afternoon. He wants to introduce his Statistical Analytical Division."

"He wants to defuse suspicions before anyone doubts what we do," Han Li said. "I wonder why we weren't told about this earlier?"

"They're smart. We would have had time to figure out an excuse not to attend if the other members of the team were there to cover for us."

"Hopefully, no one will ask us anything on statistics or analysis."

"Alexson and Connelly should be around. They'll know more than the person asking the question."

"Cray wanted Jehona to come. He says he's arranged a grand tour of the president's residence for her. However, you can stay home," Han Li told her daughter.

"I've never had a tour of the residence."

"I guess that's settled," she said, handing Moretti back his phone.

"A car will pick us up at three. Sorry to ruin your Saturday," Han Li told her daughter.

"Don't be. It will give me a chance to test this out," Jehona replied, taking the red button with the plastic protector from her pocket.

The look of surprise on Moretti and Han Li's faces caused the fifteen-year-old to laugh. "Just kidding."

The 11-mile drive to the White House took 30 minutes in the never-relenting traffic in and around the capital. Moretti wore a dark blue suit with a white shirt and blue striped tie, while Han Li was dressed in a black Brooks Brothers suit and white blouse. Both looked the part of career statisticians. The teenager sitting between them fit right in, wearing a fashionable City Studios lace-top dress.

Arriving at the White House and passing through security, they went into the residence and were greeted by Lieutenant Colonel Doug Cray, who was fashionably attired in a dark conservative suit with a red striped tie. He led them to the elevator.

"When is everyone arriving," Han Li asked as she looked around and didn't see anyone.

"They're here. The president wanted you to be the last," Cray said, holding the elevator door open until they entered and then pressing the button for the third floor. When the door opened, he pointed down the hall. "Everyone is in the Solarium."

"Do you want Jehona to wait here until the person taking her around arrives?" Han Li asked.

"She can come with us and say hi to the president first. He'd love to see her."

Upon entering the Solarium, they saw the president and the other members of Nemesis. Standing beside him in the center of the room was the Chief Justice of the United States Supreme Court.

Before Han Li knew what was happening, Moretti took her left hand and bent down on one knee. He held the wedding ring in his right hand that Jehona helped him pick out the preceding day, both leaving the house on the pretext she needed school supplies. The room became silent and closed around the couple as Moretti spoke.

"Since we've been together, you've shown me the true meaning of happiness, and I'm a better person with you at my side. Many spend their lives searching for their soul mate - their one genuine love. I'm fortunate in that I've found that person in you."

Jehona softly sobbed, and tears flowed down Han Li's cheeks. Moretti, whose eyes were getting moist, continued.

"I love you. You're the only one for me. In front of our friends and daughter, I give you my hand, heart, and love without condition - completely and forever. Will you marry me?"

Han Li gently pulled him to his feet, put a hand on each side of his face, and gave him a kiss. "Yes, I'll marry you." Jehona joined her parents, and the room erupted in applause.

The president and the other members of Nemesis stepped forward and offered their congratulations. Yan He, who had a torch going for Han Li, was the last to congratulate the couple. Even though he smiled, Moretti and Han Li would later tell each other they could see his underlying pain.

"If you're both ready," the president said, "the Chief Justice will marry you. I've taken care of the paperwork and gotten the waiting period waived." The president directed the couple to the floor-to-ceiling windows, which had a panoramic view of the Washington Monument and the Mall. The Chief Justice stepped forward and married Moretti and Han Li.

Fourteen hours later, the bride and groom landed in Athens, having decided to go there for their honeymoon and able to make a flight out of Dulles, thanks to the use of the president's helicopter. Ambassador Pullen, told by President

Ballinger that they were coming, sent an embassy car to bring them to the Grande Bretagne. President Liu arranged their stay in the Executive Grand Suite on the seventh floor, which looked out to the Acropolis, and paid their expenses as his wedding present, while President Ballinger picked up the tab for the first-class airfare. Jehona returned to boarding school in style, the president having his helicopter take her there.

Moretti and Han Li hung a "Do Not Disturb" sign on their door for three days, taking their meals from room service. On the fourth, they ventured out of the hotel and toured Athens for the next three days.

When they landed at Dulles, a government official was waiting at the aircraft's door and escorted them through the VIP section of customs and immigration. Entering the baggage claim area, they saw Cray. "You both look rested," he said, greeting the married couple. After shaking Moretti's hand, he gave Han Li a hug.

"How's our daughter?" Han Li asked.

"When the president's helicopter returned her to campus, she became quite the celebrity. The school's security is taking a much greater interest in her safety, thanks in part to a conversation the Secret Service had with them."

Since each had only a carry-on, they bypassed baggage claim and followed Cray outside.

"It's always nice to see you, but I'm guessing there's another reason you're here," Moretti said.

"What gave me away?"

"You look as nervous as an EOD rookie about to disarm a bomb."

As Cray opened the rear of the black Suburban, letting Moretti and Han Li inside first, he collapsed to the ground. Moretti, seeing blood on his jacket, pulled him inside the vehicle and closed the door as bullets bounced off its bulletproof exterior.

"Get to a hospital fast," Moretti yelled.

The driver, who saw what happened, laid rubber as he left the terminal.

"Let's see what we're dealing with," Moretti said, removing Cray's jacket and taking off his shirt with Han Li's help to look at his wound. Moretti, who had seen his fair share of gunshot wounds, examined the impact point in Cray's back but didn't find an exit wound. Trying to stem the flow of blood, he wadded a large piece of the shirt he'd torn and pressed it to the wound. "It nicked something. Call Bonaquist and tell him to alert the hospital. This doesn't look good. Every second is going to count."

Han Li got the name of the hospital that the driver was racing to and called Bonaquist.

Cray grabbed Moretti's shirt and pulled him close. "The cabal," he said in a weak voice.

"What does that mean?"

Moretti never received an answer. Seeing that Cray had a blank expression on his face, he felt his neck for a pulse. Finding none, he began CPR.

"Faster," Han Li told the driver.

The closest hospital to Dulles was StoneSprings, which was eight miles and 20 minutes away in light traffic. With the government vehicle's flashing lights and siren, the driver made it in ten.

Moretti got Cray's heart to beat again, but his pulse was almost nonexistent. When the driver pulled in front of the emergency room entrance, four medical staff waited beside a gurney. They rushed Cray inside.

Moretti and Han Li sat in the waiting room, Moretti telling her what Cray said.

"The cabal?"

"I don't know what that means, but I'm going to find out. When I do, I'm going to kill everyone who had a hand in this," Moretti said in a stern voice.

"Mind if I help?

AUTHOR'S NOTES

This is a work of fiction. The characters within do not represent nor are they meant to implicate anyone in the actual world. That said, substantial portions of *The Forgotten*, as stated below, are factual.

The author first got the idea for this latest Matt Moretti-Han Li novel after reading an article indicating human traffickers use Greece as a central European portal to move their victims to other destinations within the EU. Most of the data that Hellenic Police Colonel Defrim Kote provided Ambassador Kyle Pullen is from: https://www.state.gov/j/tip/rls/tiprpt/countries/2014/226730.htm; https://www.dosomething.org/us/facts/11-facts-about-human-trafficking; https://www.humanrightsfirst.org/resource/human-trafficking-numbers; https://neutrinodata.s3.amazonaws.com/a21/userimages/TheProblem.pdf.

Profits derived from human trafficking vary depending on which article one reads. The author went with $31.6 billion, which was in line with most estimates. Trafficking in children has risen 27 percent in recent years, with one out of every three victims a boy. Prosecution of those engaged in trafficking has not been meaningful. Statistically, of the 132 countries monitored by the United Nations Office on Drugs and Crime, 16 percent have not convicted a single person for this crime. Sadly, only one to two percent of European victims get rescued, and only one in one hundred thousand of those involved in European human trafficking are convicted.

As mentioned, Kolonaki is an elegant area of stately neighborhoods, parks, and gardens, which is a short walk from the Grande Bretagne hotel. Aside from the luxury shopping, it has beautiful neighborhood restaurants, many with outdoor seating. The Relanti restaurant in Kolonaki exists and has fantastic food.

The description of Greek coffee is accurate. Prepared in a briki, it's potent and served with foam on top and grounds at the bottom. Taste-wise, it's the same as Turkish coffee. When the author asked a server whether only special forces were tough enough to drink it without sugar, he didn't receive a response. My bad.

My apologies to the Mystique hotel in Santorini for the missile attack. It goes without saying that the hotel's ownership, past or present, is not associated with the US ambassador to Greece. The author established that connection for the storyline. The Mystique is the author's favorite hotel in Santorini and provides its guests with an extraordinary level of hospitality, excellent food, and a stunning view of the Aegean Sea. It's on the southernmost tip of Oia. When you're there, ask Sokratis to make you a Mojito or an Aperol Spritz—you'll never have better.

What the Mystique is to Santorini, the Grande Bretagne is to Athens. In the center of the city, the hotel dates from 1874 and has a hypnotizing view of the Acropolis, especially from its rooftop restaurant.

The Omonoia Square area of Athens is as described, although there are indications it's becoming somewhat safer. While the square itself is not the most dangerous section, because of the many highways that lead to it, the backstreets around it are. It's especially dangerous at night. The author walked this area while conducting his research and found that it had more than its fair share of junkies, prostitutes, and homeless.

The *Green Seas, Green Harbor, Green Island, and Green Port* are fictional ships and not meant to depict another vessel that bears that name.

The description and technical information on the rocket-propelled grenade (RPG) and the Serbian Advanced Light Attack System (ALAS) missile are accurate. The fictional ALAS missile attack on the US embassy in Athens was inspired by an actual RPG attack by a group calling itself *Revolutionary Struggle.* This occurred on the morning of January 12, 2007. There were no fatalities or injuries.

The budget given for the Department of Defense, discretionary and mandatory, is accurate. The DOD budget that's referenced can be seen at: https://dod.defense.gov/News/SpecialReports/Budget2019.aspx

The USS *Marco Island* is a fictional amphibious carrier, although its description is based on an America-class amphibious assault ship.

Kymi is on the Greek island of Euboea and is accurately described. However, to the best of the author's knowledge, it's not a smuggling hub, nor are any of their police officers bent. These accusations were made for the sake of the storyline. If you have an opportunity to go Euboea - take it! Besides an incredible view of the Aegean Sea, the city is one of the greenest in the country, and its beaches are considered by many to be the most pristine. Besides tourism, Agriculture supports the local economy, its principal exports being figs, cherries, and olive oil.

The Caves of the Lakes is accurately described, except for the dimensions of the entrance, the circular chamber within, and the exit that Gashi and Manjani took to escape.

The author has eaten at the Thalami restaurant in Oia many times. Family-owned, it has excellent food and outstanding service. I couldn't get away from ordering their souvlaki, which was served with toasted pita bread and French fries - two of my favorite foods.

The Russian government purportedly uses SP-117 during interrogations. It's tasteless, odorless, colorless, has no side effects, and the drug's recipient has no recollection of the interrogation. The Russians primarily employ it on their overseas agents to ensure they haven't been "turned."

There is no indication of corruption within the Greek government. This was used for the sake of the storyline as the author needed members of the government, police officers, and the judiciary to be on Tosku's payroll. Interestingly, the author discovered during his research that the government considers its most serious form of corruption, for the economically strapped country, to be the nonpayment of taxes. In contrast, the citizens of Greece look upon tax avoidance as a national sport.

Bezmer Airbase is a joint US-Bulgarian airfield that the military views as one of its six essential airbases outside the continental US. It's 58 miles west of Burgas.

The reference to the JFK Special Warfare Center and School at the Yuma Proving Grounds in Arizona, and the RA-1 parachute, is accurate. Preparation for Moretti and Han Li's leap out of the C-130 was obtained from http://balestales.com/jump-commands/ and https://trello.com/c/91XvoJd7/10-jump-commands. The equipment described in the HAHO jump is accurate. You can find further details at https://www.cryeprecision.com/ and https://cpsworld.com/ products/accessories/haho-thermal-suit/.

The *USS Ohio* was originally a nuclear-powered fleet ballistic missile submarine converted to a guided missile submarine and re-designated SSGN-726. The technical information given for this vessel is accurate. However, its incursion into Bulgarian waters and its rendezvous with a Chinese navy submarine is fictional and done for the storyline. It was a convenient method of transporting Behar Tosku to the black prison in Mohe, China.

The Changzheng 6 submarine exists. However, it's not believed to operate within the Mediterranean Sea or the Arabian Sea. Most military naval experts believe the Chinese keep their SLBMs in waters near their coast where domestic naval and air forces can protect them. The JL-3 is a relatively new missile that replaced the JL-2. The author gave the Chinese navy the benefit of the doubt that the Changzheng 6 carried the latest weaponry.

As stated in the author's past novels, Mohe is the northernmost town in China, with only a river separating it from Siberia. The author, who lives in Florida, was there one February wearing every piece of warm gear he owned. It was -26 degrees Fahrenheit without the wind. The black prison in Mohe may or may not exist, although if you drive from the airport to the city halfway between you'll see a complex that resembles a prison to your left. Watch towers and high walls topped with barbed wire make that a reasonable assumption. To the best of the author's knowledge, a Chinese airbase doesn't exist in Mohe, although the airport can easily accommodate military aircraft.

ACKNOWLEDGMENTS

An author's manuscript is not only the result of their hard work and inspiration but reflects the passion breathed into it by friends and family. I'm fortunate to have a wonderful family and an extraordinary group of friends who unselfishly give me the benefit of their opinions and thoughts. Sometimes their advice scarred my ego-but I heal well.

To Kerry Refkin, for her invaluable recommendations on my storyline and for assisting with the edits. Your insights and perceptions are extraordinary.

To Lowell & Sally Senitz, founders of Wings of Shelter, an organization that operates safe houses in Southwest Florida for minor females rescued from domestic sex trafficking. They help rehabilitate these survivors through a victim's centered, non-punitive approach and understand the complications of long-term abuse, neglect, manipulation, and the brainwashing that they've endured. They train their staff to understand post-traumatic Stress Disorder (PTSD) and its effects. This organization also empowers and encourages these survivors academically, emotionally, spiritually, and socially to heal the complex trauma that they've endured, to move them toward independence. Their program residents receive trauma-focused mental health counseling, medical care, private schooling, tutoring, the opportunity to pursue extracurricular hobbies, part-time jobs, and re-socialization through a volunteer big sister program (www.wingsofshelter.com).

To the group - Scott Cray, Dr. Charles and Aprille Pappas, Dr. John and Cindy Cancelliere, Doug and Winnie Ballinger, Alexandra Parra, Ed Houck, Cheryl Rinell, Mark Iwinski, Mike Calbot, and Dr. Meir Daller for continuing to be my sounding boards.

To: Zhang Jingjie for her research. No one is better at finding that needle in the haystack.

To Dr. Kevin Hunter and Rob Durst, the author's close friends for decades, for making cybersecurity, IT, and computer hardware and software comprehensible.

To Clay Parker and Jim Bonaquist. Thank you for the great legal advice you continue to provide.

To Bill Wiltshire and Debbie Layport. Thanks again for your superb financial and accounting skills.

To our friends-Zoran Avramoski, Piotr Cretu, Neti Gaxholli, and Aleksandar Toporovski. Thanks for your insights.

To Doug and Winnie Ballinger and Scott and Betty Cray – my ongoing thanks for all you do for the countless people who cannot fend for themselves.

To the incredible staff of the Mystique Hotel-the general manager, Alexandra, Michaela, Dimitra, Maxim, Sokratis, and others who make every guest's stay memorable. You all take hospitality to another level.

ABOUT THE AUTHOR

Alan Refkin is the author of six previous works of fiction and the co-author of four business books on China, for which he received the Editor's Choice Award for *The Wild Wild East,* and for *Piercing the Great Wall of Corporate China.* The author and his wife, Kerry, live in southwest Florida, where he's currently working on his next Matt Moretti-Han Li novel. More information on the author, including his blogs and newsletters, can be obtained at *alanrefkin.com.*